I have a surprise for you. . . .

The door opened.

"Welcome."

The nurse stood before her. She looked different from before. On her cheeks were two bright spots of red, and her mouth was a crimson slash across her face.

"I'm so glad you're here, Alicia dear. I have a surprise for you."

She held a jacket out toward Alicia. "Go on, dear. Put it on. It was made for you."

Alicia looked at the jacket. There was something strange about it. Then she understood what was wrong. *It was a straitjacket.*

Alicia started to scream, but when she opened her mouth, no sound came out.

Other Scholastic Thrillers
you will enjoy:

AMNESIA

**SINCLAIR
SMITH**

SCHOLASTIC INC.
New York Toronto London Auckland Sydney

ISBN 0-590-50952-7

Copyright © 1996 by Dona Smith.
All rights reserved. Published by Scholastic Inc.

12 11 10 9 8 7 6 5 4 3 2 1   6 7 8 9/9 0 1/0

Printed in the U.S.A.   01

First Scholastic printing, January 1996

For Philomena

AMNESIA

Chapter 1

A jagged scream slashed the silent fabric of the night.

The girl sat up suddenly, dazed, as if her mind had been rocketed back from some far-away place. She clutched the covers around her.

It was so dark! For a moment she thought she had forgotten to open her eyes. But her eyes were wide, straining. The velvet curtain of night so shrouded her it was as if she were blind.

The scream came again, ripping through the darkness.

Fear's cold knife edge streaked down the girl's spine. Her heart pounded. She wanted to run, but she could not see — and she was paralyzed with fear. Her mind reeled, trying to grasp onto something — anything — to steady itself.

Then another scream tore through the darkness and everything became suddenly, horrifyingly clear.

The person who is screaming is me.

I don't know who I am.

Chapter 2

I don't know who I am.

The knowledge was overwhelming — and horrible. A yawning black chasm of fear opened up inside. She felt herself plummeting down, down into the depths of it, into a void. Her mouth opened and her ears rang with the sound of her terror.

Suddenly there was the sound of feet rushing in the hallway, rushing toward her, growing louder and louder. Voices. Then a brilliant flash of light. It shone everywhere, blinding her.

Strong hands gripped her arms, pulling at her. She struggled, thrashed at the unseen beings who wrestled with her. She had not thought it would be possible to be more afraid.

Then something sharp pricked her arm, made her draw in her breath with surprise and pain.

Darkness gathered again. Everything was fading, fading away as she tried desperately to hold on. She was falling, falling dizzily into the blackness. She swirled around and around, whirling downward. . . .

And then she dreamed. In the dream she was in a long, dark tunnel. She was trying to run toward the light, but she knew that someone didn't want her to make it. She was being chased by a shadowy figure with fierce, blazing eyes. If it caught her something too terrible to imagine would happen.

As the figure chased her, it was shouting something. . . . What was it?

Was it threatening?

Or *accusing*?

She couldn't understand the words. They were distorted and strange, as when something happened to the sound at the movies.

It seemed the longer she ran, the longer the tunnel became. The light seemed farther and farther away. And whoever was behind her got closer and closer, until she could feel the hot breath of her pursuer on her neck . . . and then pain exploded in her head.

The girl opened her eyes. At first it seemed she was looking up through murky water at a light that was far away. But soon things became clearer and clearer. Finally everything snapped into focus. The tunnel had been a dream. But the pain in her head was real.

It was white everywhere. Sound at first was still muffled, as if she had cotton in her ears. Gradually, sounds sharpened. So did the pain.

Someone was singing tunelessly, repeating the same passage again and again, *tra-la-la, tra-la-la*. A figure in white. *An angel?* the girl wondered for a moment.

No, her senses told her instantly. The scent she was breathing was disinfectant. Of course, this was a hospital. The angel in white was a nurse.

Well, at least I'm not dead, she said to herself. Even if I don't know who I am.

"*Tra-la-la, tra-la-la,*" sang the nurse.

Ever so slowly, the girl turned her head to the right a little. There was another bed in the room. But it was empty.

Why do I know this is a hospital, when I can't remember my name? I can't remember if I'm old or young, short or tall, pretty or plain.

What is my favorite color? What do I like to do, and who do I love? Where is my family?

It was all so incredibly astonishing that your life could simply vanish, like a slate that had been erased.

The girl found that the pain had lessened from a sharp scream in her skull to a dull, steady buzz. Maybe I'm just getting used to it, she thought.

She started to swing her legs over the side of the bed, but stopped abruptly as a white-hot flash of pain shot from her right ankle up to her knee and then exploded through her entire body. A noise came out of her mouth that was a scream and a groan at the same time.

The *tra-la-la*-ing stopped abruptly. The nurse came running over, a look of concern on her pale, doughy features. She moved so quickly that her nurse's cap tilted on her gray head.

"Oh, you're finally awake," she said, looking down at the girl. "Be careful, dear. That ankle was badly twisted. Are you all right?"

The question struck the girl as rather funny. If I was all right, why would I be in the hospital? she said to herself.

But she looked at the nurse and nodded. "Yes," she said softly. It was difficult to speak. Her tongue felt thick and fuzzy. Her lips felt rubbery. "I'm all right," she added, wanting to practice speaking. It felt as if she hadn't done it in a long time.

The nurse's face lit up like an electrified smiley button. "Of *course* you're all right. You're in the Grady County Hospital."

"Grady?" the girl echoed, wanting the name to become familiar. It didn't.

"Well, I'll go get the doctor." The nurse bustled away, reminding the girl of a waitress who had just said, "Your cherry pie will be coming right up. Have a nice day."

Moments later, a tired-looking young woman wearing a white doctor's coat entered. Her auburn hair was pinned up off her neck. Several strands had escaped and hung untidily about her face. Her gray eyes were as expressionless as two clams.

"Hello, Alicia. I'm Dr. Kellogg," she said.

My name is Alicia. The girl drank in the information greedily, like a thirsty runner after a long race.

"At least, I'm assuming your name is Alicia," continued the doctor. "That's the name on the bracelet you were wearing when you were brought in. It's in the drawer beside your bed."

Alicia opened the drawer and took the bracelet out. It was a deep-blue leather band.

On its surface the name *Alicia* was stamped in intricate letters. It's the only way I know my name, she thought. *How strange.* She replaced the bracelet in the drawer.

"We've been waiting for you to wake up," the doctor said. "Now just relax." She bent down, shone a light in Alicia's eyes, and stood up again before Alicia could pull away.

"So," Dr. Kellogg said briskly, "how do you feel?"

"My head hurts, and I can't remember . . ." Alicia's voice trailed off.

The doctor smiled. When she spoke, it was as if she thought completely forgetting who you were was barely worthy of notice.

"I know you've suffered memory loss. You talked about it when you were first admitted." She glanced at Alicia and chuckled. "Although you may not remember."

Alicia got the joke — she just didn't feel like laughing.

"Anyway," the doctor continued, "you said that your name was Alicia, you remembered that much. You got banged around a lot, but it's nothing serious. And don't worry" — the smile broadened — "it's nothing that will affect that pretty face."

The doctor thrust a round mirror into her hands. "Look in the mirror."

Numbly, Alicia took the mirror and stared into it. The face reflected back at her was pale, with prominent cheekbones and large, violet eyes. Dark brown hair fell to her shoulders. There were deep, purplish-red circles under her eyes.

For a moment, panic threatened to overwhelm her. She turned to the doctor and tried to say something, but her tongue moved clumsily, as if coated thickly with wool padding.

"Don't be alarmed, those dark circles under your eyes will fade," the doctor said with a jolly smile of encouragement. "You'll look just like a model."

Alicia opened her mouth to tell the doctor she wasn't worried about looking like a model, she was worried about not recognizing her own face, but the doctor held up her hand for silence. "You'd better get some more rest now." She glanced at her watch. "I've got to go. See you soon."

Dr. Kellogg was gone before Alicia was even able to form any of the questions that were hurtling around her mind. What kind of accident did I have? What happened?

Alicia stared into the mirror again. "You'll look just like a model." Dr. Kellogg's words echoed in her head. What good was looking like a model if you didn't know who you were? she thought sourly.

As Alicia looked into the mirror, she fought to control the rising tide of panic that threatened to engulf her.

If this is my face, why don't I know it? she asked herself. Her thoughts whirled in confusion. The eyes that stared back at her were no more familiar than the eyes of a stranger. She wanted to run from the room, screaming, "You've made a terrible mistake! This isn't my face — this is someone else! Give me back the face that I know! Give it back!"

Chapter 3

Three days went by, and yet when Alicia looked in the mirror she still had to remind herself that the face that looked back at her was her own. Even her name was scarcely more familiar. She was becoming more used to responding when someone said it. Still, she wore her identity like borrowed clothing — it didn't feel as if it was really hers.

"Hello, Alicia dear."

"Hello."

Nurse Tra-la-la, who she had learned was named Nurse Stewart ("Call me Annabel"), bustled in and set up the tray for breakfast, singing to herself and smiling all the while. Then she bustled out, humming her same tra-la-la. Alicia decided that even though she knew her name was Stewart, she would still always be Nurse Tra-la-la.

Alicia sighed and stared at the ceiling. I'm in such a terrible mess, she said to herself. Each night as she waited for sleep, she prayed that when she awoke her ordeal would be over, and she would know who she was. Each morning she opened her eyes and everything was still the same.

In the days that had passed, Alicia had been examined, tested, and questioned until she didn't think she could take it anymore. There were times she'd been sure she would have run screaming out of the hospital — if only her ankle didn't hurt so much.

Always, there were the same questions. *What do you remember about the accident? What do you remember about the day it happened?*

Always she gave the same answer. *Nothing.*

If only I could remember something, some tiny piece of anything, perhaps the awful, fearful feeling that haunts me would relax and loosen its grip for a while, she thought.

No one here could give her much information to help her remember. She'd been found wandering on the highway covered with blood. Someone had called an ambulance, which brought her to the hospital. That's all anybody knew.

"Hi, Alicia. How are you doing today?" Dr. Kellogg's voice pulled Alicia from her brooding thoughts. As always, the doctor sounded a little breathless, and looked a little stressed. But sooner or later that game-show hostess smile, which made Alicia feel so uneasy, appeared.

I don't like this place, Alicia said to herself. Everyone is always in such a hurry, and they look so tired.

Yet they're always wearing big smiles. Smiling when they don't mean it, and chuckling and laughing — when nothing is funny.

It made Alicia think they were hiding something from her.

"You're awfully quiet today, Alicia," the doctor said, tilting her head to one side.

"I don't have anything to say," Alicia replied curtly. Then she added, "Don't ask me if I remember anything, because I don't. If I did, I'd speak up and tell you."

She punched the mattress in frustration. "It's not fair! A bump on the head and my whole life is taken away from me."

The game-show smile vanished from the doctor's face. She looked truly sympathetic and concerned.

"I know it must be hard for you," she said

quietly. Then she crossed her arms and looked thoughtful.

"You know, Alicia — although you were in an accident, there is a possibility that the real cause of your amnesia isn't physical at all. Perhaps it's because of something that happened that's so hard to face you don't *want* to remember it.

Alicia glanced up sharply. It was almost as if the doctor had been reading her thoughts.

"Is that often the case?"

Dr. Kellogg looked as if she was considering her words carefully. "There have been many cases when an upsetting occurrence was the cause of amnesia. And there have been many instances when the cause was something else. We know you hit your head, but that's not necessarily the reason for the memory loss. Sometimes amnesia means there's something you're afraid to remember."

Dr. Kellogg seemed about to say something else when she cast a hurried look at her watch. Whatever she was going to say was forgotten. "Darn! I've got a staff meeting soon."

For a moment, the doctor looked flustered. Apparently she realized it, and composed her features. Once more, her face wore the pasted-on smile. The whole transformation was so instantaneous Alicia couldn't decide if it was eerie . . . or comical.

"Anyway," Dr. Kellogg said brightly, "your memory just might get better before your ankle does. You never know."

The doctor laid a hand on Alicia's shoulder. "I wish I wasn't in such a hurry, because I have wonderful news for you." Incredibly, her smile grew wider. Without knowing why, Alicia felt her stomach knot into a tight ball of apprehension.

"The good news is that you don't have to stay in the hospital anymore."

Alicia stared at the doctor's smiling face. The full meaning of her words slowly penetrated her consciousness.

"You can't mean it! Where would I go?" she burst out. "I don't have any money — and I don't even remember who my family is. You can't make me leave the hospital!"

Dr. Kellogg shook her head slowly, with exaggerated calmness. "Alicia, you've got to stop being such a worrier! Everything's going to be fine! You didn't let me finish. What I was going to say is that we've found your . . . family. Your sister has been looking for you and now she's found you. She's come to take you home and help you recover. She'll be in any minute now."

This news caught Alicia completely off guard. Stunned, she realized she'd never considered the possibility of a brother or sister.

I have a sister. She tried to let the knowledge sink in. A wave of relief swept over her. Someone knew her! She could leave this place! Her sister would take her home.

"She's coming here now?"

The doctor nodded, beaming. "She's the one who told us your name was Alicia *Taylor*. You live right here in Grady County, in a little town called Grimly."

Alicia paid no attention to the name of the town. "My sister will take me to my family," she breathed. "Oh, I wonder if I'll remember them?"

Dr. Kellogg's smile faded slightly. "One thing at a time. Don't expect too much."

"Oh. Of course." Alicia was disappointed at having her enthusiasm dampened.

But it sprang back instantly. Her sister would be here soon! Anticipation surged through her veins. She reached for the comb and mirror on the bedside table. As she moved, she felt a twinge of pain in her ankle, but she was too excited to pay much attention to it. She began combing her hair quickly.

I hope I recognize her, she prayed. Perhaps when I see her, memories will come flooding back. Maybe I'll even remember who I am.

"Alicia."

Alicia knew the voice didn't belong to Dr. Kellogg. She looked up from the mirror and her eyes fastened on the figure who was standing at the foot of her hospital bed. The figure was cloaked in black from head to toe.

"Alicia. I've been so worried about you." The figure spoke again, but Alicia couldn't see the mouth moving. The voice was husky and low, almost a whisper.

"Oh, look — here's your sister!" Dr. Kellogg exclaimed.

The shadowy figure moved to the side of Alicia's bed. Dark glittering eyes stared out at her. "I'm your sister Marta."

Alicia stared back at the glittering eyes and was suddenly engulfed in a feeling of overwhelming terror. "No . . ." Alicia whispered. "Stay away from me."

She slid back toward the wall, the movement setting off the pain in her ankle afresh.

In her panic, Alicia didn't feel a thing.

"You're not my sister! I know who you are. I've seen you before! You're not my sister!"

Alicia was face-to-face with the figure who had chased her in her dreams.

Chapter 4

A tense, heavy silence hung in the air. Alicia's eyes darted back and forth between the figure that called itself her sister Marta and Dr. Kellogg.

"Alicia, calm down. You're letting your imagination run away with you," Dr. Kellogg said.

Alicia pressed her back against the wall. Her heart pounded in her chest. The doctor doesn't sound very calm, she thought. She heard the acid edge of tension in her voice.

What kind of nightmare am I in? she wondered. A figure had just walked out of her nightmare and was standing close enough to touch her.

As Alicia sat still as a statue, the figure began to unwind pieces of the shadowy blackness from around itself. In seconds Alicia realized they were only scarves.

Finally, the figure removed the black hat that had been pulled down low over the forehead. Now the figure became a tall, big-boned young woman with deep brown eyes and a face with a wide forehead framed with wavy brown hair.

The doctor was right, Alicia thought. My imagination ran away with me. This was a person, after all. It was not the dark figure with blazing eyes from her dream. The figure was a creation of fantasy. Her terror drained away.

"I'm sorry," she said, feeling her taut muscles go limp with relief. "I saw you wrapped up in that hat and scarves and you reminded me of something I saw in a dream. . . ." Alicia let her voice trail off. She felt silly about screaming like a frightened child in the dark.

"That's okay," Marta said, putting her hat and scarf on the chair. "It's a little cold for March. I guess I do look pretty scary wrapped up like that." She smiled. "Well, now do I look familiar?"

Alicia had absolutely no recognition of her. She could have been anyone — including a complete stranger. She's my sister, and we don't even look the least bit alike, she thought as she looked back at Marta.

"I don't remember you," she said with a shake of her head.

"Don't worry, the memory will come," Marta said, her eyes looking into Alicia's.

Well, at least she isn't grinning and chuckling at me in the patronizing way the doctors and nurses do, Alicia thought, deciding a point in Marta's favor.

"I'll let you two be alone for a while. I've got to dash," said Dr. Kellogg. "Now Alicia, everything will be just *fine*, so you relax."

When the doctor reached the door, she turned around. "You know what might be fun for the two of you? When you get home, maybe your sister can take you for a haircut. I think a nice short style would look good."

Her comment left Alicia speechless. After a moment, the doctor shrugged, then turned around and left.

The tension level in the room dropped as soon as the doctor was gone. "Relax!" echoed Alicia. "I can't remember who I am, and she tells me to take it easy! What an idea!"

She propped herself up on her elbows. "Have you noticed that they have kind of a strange bedside manner here?" She grinned broadly and did a perfect imitation of Dr. Kellogg. " 'Hey, so you're in a hospital. Things couldn't be better! Honey, you've got to do something about that hair!' Sometimes I'm not sure if she knows whether she's a doctor or a beautician."

Alicia started laughing in spite of herself. Marta looked at her quizzically for a moment, and then she started laughing, too.

Marta has an unusual kind of laugh, Alicia thought. It was kind of a hiccup.

When the laughter died, Marta faced Alicia with a somber expression. "Do you remember *anything* about what happened?"

There was that question again. "No. Everybody's been asking that over and over again. I'll tell you the same thing that I tell them. No."

A single, hiccuping laugh issued from Marta's lips. Then a look of surprise crossed her features as if she wondered where the laugh came from. "I'm sorry," she said. "I don't know why I laughed. I don't think it's funny."

An expression of seriousness settled like a cloud over her features. She crossed her arms over her chest, walked to the window, and looked out. Without looking at Alicia, she said,

"You mean you really remember nothing?"

"I said I didn't. I was hoping *you* could tell *me* something."

Marta was silent. She just kept looking out the window. The more the silence deepened, the more apprehensive Alicia became. What *wasn't* Marta saying? Each second that ticked by became an eternity.

Marta was so quiet and still — as if she had gone off somewhere in her mind. "Marta, there must be something you can tell me about what happened," Alicia prompted.

Alicia watched as Marta blinked several times. She stood up straighter. It was as if she was returning from wherever she had gone in her thoughts. Finally, she began to speak. "You know . . ."

"*Tra-la-la.* Isn't it wonderful that you two have found each other?" Nurse Tra-la-la hurried in with the breakfast tray. "You two must have so much to catch up on. *Tra-la-la.*"

She put the tray down across Alicia's bed. Smiling, as usual, she tore open a small packet of instant coffee and poured it into a cup. Then she poured in hot water from a small glass container. "Some problem with the coffee urns," she said. "But this instant is very good."

"I'm sure I'll think I'm drinking fresh perked," Alicia said dryly.

The nurse glanced up and looked from Alicia to Marta, and back to Alicia, and saw the tension on their faces. Her smile vanished. "Oh, my," she murmured. "I won't intrude on you two. I can see you have a lot to talk about." Then, without another word, she hurried from the room.

"She's right, you know," Alicia said quietly when the nurse was gone. "We have a lot to talk about." She clasped her hands together.

Carefully, she pushed the tray away, then pulled the covers back and turned, slowly lowering her feet to the floor. She sat on the edge of the bed and looked at Marta earnestly.

"Well, go ahead and tell me something. It doesn't much matter where you start, since I don't know *anything*."

Marta pressed her lips together in a thin line. "All right," she said, finally. "Let's get you out of this hospital first, and then we can have a long talk. But I warn you. You're not going to like some of the things you're going to hear."

Chapter 5

"There's hardly any traffic. Isn't that wonderful!" Marta said without taking her eyes off the road.

Alicia looked at her for a moment, startled by the enthusiasm in her tone. *Too much enthusiasm,* she thought. Marta turned and gave her a warm smile.

"Sometimes, this road is so *congested,*" Marta said in the same bright, smiley tone. While she went on about the traffic, Alicia tuned her out. She wondered how much longer Marta would go on about trivialities before getting down to what was really important, namely the events surrounding Alicia's arrival in the hospital.

Soon she was lost in her own thoughts. Barely an hour ago, I didn't even know I had a sister. Now here we are, on the highway headed for home, she said to herself. What would *home* be like?

Alicia stared out the window at the scenery whizzing by. She kept hoping for a spark of recognition that didn't come.

"Okay," she said, turning to Marta after they had ridden in silence for a while. "You promised to tell me everything once we were on the way home. Well, here we are."

Alicia saw Marta's jaw tense, and she gripped the steering wheel tighter, so that her knuckles whitened.

"There's something they didn't tell you at the hospital that might come as a bit of a shock." Marta glanced at Alicia. "I hope you won't be upset." She took a deep breath.

"You mentioned that your whole life had changed in a few days — but it's not a few days, Alicia. You've been in a coma for four months."

Alicia drew her breath in sharply, and then blurted, "Four months! It's not possible! When I woke up I thought that I'd been sleeping for a long time — and nobody told me any different. Why didn't they tell me? And why didn't you tell me when we were at the hospital?"

The car jolted over a pothole. "Oopsie daisy!" Marta gasped in surprise. The expression sounded strange and jarring to Alicia's ears. When Marta recovered herself, she said, "At the hospital they told me not to give you any news that might upset you. Perhaps they were wrong."

"Wrong," echoed Alicia, feeling betrayed. She had lost four months of her life, and no one had told her — until now. She slumped back against the seat for a moment. Then she sat up straight.

"It appears I have a lot of catching up to do, so we might as well start. Tell me about myself. What do I like to do? Do I have a best friend?"

"Sure." Marta smiled at her warmly. Her face practically *lit up*. "One thing I can tell you is that *we* have a great relationship. We're about as close as two sisters can be. We're practically inseparable."

"Good." Alicia nodded. "But, do I have a best friend?"

The smile faded from Marta's lips. "You have other friends, I suppose. You never talked about them. It always seemed that *we* were best friends."

Alicia heard the hurt in Marta's voice. "I'm sorry if there are some important things I don't remember."

After a moment Marta shrugged. "That's okay. It's not your fault," she said tightly. "You'll remember soon enough. On to the next question."

Her understanding made Alicia feel guiltier than ever. She took a deep breath. "Am I popular? Do I have a boyfriend?"

Marta's profile drooped. "Those things weren't very important to you. People always liked you, but you've always been kind of shy, on the quiet side. You preferred to keep to yourself and spend time doing things at home."

"Really? What things?"

Marta's smile returned. "We spend a lot of time together, talking, playing games like checkers, chess, cards. You love to play *Hearts*. Oh, and we do crossword puzzles a lot, too."

"Oh." Alicia drummed her fingers on the dashboard and looked out the window at the road.

Marta went on talking. "We never went out much. We were always happy at home, with each other."

Alicia exhaled in a long sigh. "Well, how about you? Do you go to school, or have a job?"

The question had barely left Alicia's lips when Marta piped up, "I'm an executive with a company downtown. It's a big job, but it's really very boring. It's nothing to talk about."

In spite of what Marta said about the job being boring, a little smile was playing about her lips. She looks quite pleased with herself, Alicia thought. "I'm sure you're being modest about your job," Alicia said. "It must be very interesting. Tell me about it," she prompted.

Marta's reaction surprised her. "No," she said, shortly. "It's a big executive position, all right. But it's dull. I don't like talking about my job." She tapped her thick fingers on the steering wheel.

"Oh," Alicia said, and sighed again. Everything about their lives sounded so bland, so dull, so dreary. I'm just finding out about myself and already I wish I were somebody else, she thought.

Marta turned off the highway. They drove through one of the streets of the small town, past a park.

"This is Grimly," Marta said, her voice once again bright with enthusiasm. Once more Alicia searched for something she recognized, but found nothing. The town was very small and went by in a blur. In moments they had entered the town, driven through, and were on their way out.

"It's not a very big town," Marta said, stating the obvious. They drove on past a tiny shopping center with a pizzeria at one end. Moments later Marta turned onto a narrow street, then turned again onto another street that ended in a little circle. There was an old-fashioned frame house, painted gray, at the end.

"Here's the house," Marta said. She turned to Alicia with a wide smile on her face. "It's so great to have you home." She maneuvered the car into the driveway beside the house.

Alicia noticed that the yard was unkempt. The grass was spotty and dotted with weeds.

Marta pulled the car into a small, dark garage. "Shouldn't our parents' car be here?" Alicia asked.

Marta stopped the car and sat staring straight ahead. She didn't look at Alicia, whose senses suddenly went on alert. "Our parents are here, aren't they?" asked Alicia.

When Marta still said nothing, a warning bell began to sound in Alicia's brain. It was faint at first, but quickly grew louder and louder.

"Marta, they're here, aren't they?" she repeated. "Why don't I see their car? Why don't they come out?" Alicia spoke faster and faster. Her voice took on a strained, high-pitched squeak.

Marta put her head in her hands. "I'm so sorry, Alicia. I tried to tell you sooner — but this is hard for me, too."

"What?" Alicia's nerves were stretched taut to the breaking point. Her eyes, growing accustomed to the dimness of the garage, darted nervously around, taking in its untidiness, the handful of odd cans and rusty tools on the shelves. She heard the sound of her own breathing, coming in short, shallow gasps.

She knew, *knew* that what Marta was going to say would be horrible — unthinkable. Time slowed as she waited. She prayed it would stop. But it didn't.

"I told you that there were things you wouldn't want to hear, Alicia." Marta raised her head and looked at Alicia. Her eyes glittered wetly. "Our parents are dead. They died in the same car accident that put you in the hospital."

Chapter 6

Marta opened the door that led from the garage to the kitchen and stepped aside. "Go on in, Alicia. You're home." Her face was lit up in a wide grin that Alicia found strange, considering she had been talking about their parents' deaths only moments ago.

I've been in a coma for months. She's had time to adjust, she reminded herself. Her mind was numb with shock at the news. The excitement she felt only a few moments ago at the thought of entering her new home had vanished.

She had such an eerie feeling of unreality. She was sorry her parents were dead, and yet she could not grieve for them . . . because she didn't even remember them.

"Come on in," Marta urged.

Alicia took a deep breath and stepped into

the kitchen. It was scarcely brighter than the garage. The shades were pulled down, and the curtains closed. They were green, with ruffles.

Looking around, she saw it was a plain sort of room, not dismal perhaps, but certainly not cheery. Nondescript was the word that fit, she decided.

The cabinets were white, the walls painted green. The floor was black and white linoleum squares. In one corner hulked a large, ancient-looking refrigerator. Nothing looked familiar.

"Come on and have a look at the living room," Marta said, leading the way.

Limping, Alicia followed her into a room that was darker than the kitchen. Heavy drapes were pulled shut, blocking out all but a few thin fingers of light that filtered through. The effect was like being in a cave.

She maneuvered herself painfully over to the windows. "It's so dark in here," she exclaimed, pulling at the heavy drapes. After a moment of examination, she found the cord to pull them back. "There, that's better!"

"The sun fades the furniture," Marta said stiffly. She began pulling the drapes closed again.

"Marta, wait! I can't remember anything if

I can't see it," Alicia cried. "Besides — it's creepy to have all the sunlight shut out of the room. It's like we're hiding or something."

Marta hesitated. After a moment, she released the drapery pull. "Well, it's not good for the furniture," she said again. She fixed Alicia with a narrow gaze of disapproval.

Alicia ignored her and turned to look around the living room. The mantel was adorned with an ornate brass clock. There were several overstuffed chairs in the room, each with a scarf of crocheted lace over the back and on each arm.

The rugs were deep burgundy oriental, and all of the wood was dark mahogany. Every available surface was covered with porcelain figurines of people or animals.

It was the overall appearance of the room, rather than any detail, that created the most startling impression. It was something out of a time warp. The kind of room you would see in old movies. The eyes of the porcelain figurines seemed to be silently vigilant, staring at her.

"Some of these pieces are collector's items," Marta said, her voice full of pride. She gestured toward a figure of a sleeping dog. "This one's a hundred years old."

"It's nice," Alicia said, not knowing what else to say. The figure of the dog didn't look antique to her — it didn't even look very interesting. One thing, though. It wasn't dusty. In spite of the myriad of knickknacks, there wasn't a speck of dust anywhere in the room. "You really keep the place in top shape," she said. "With a demanding job, you must have someone to help with the cleaning." If you do, maybe the person will help me remember something, she thought.

But Marta was shaking her head. "Goodness no," she exclaimed, with a shocked expression. "I wouldn't dream of it. I do it all myself. That way I know it's done right."

Before Alicia had time to comment, Marta said, "You must be hungry."

Suddenly, Alicia realized that she *was* famished. As if on cue, there was a rumbling in her stomach. "As a matter of fact, I'm starved," she said, running her hand along the arm of an overstuffed chair. It felt velvety, but not familiar.

Marta disappeared into the kitchen. Alicia heard the sound of her walking across the linoleum floor. She heard the refrigerator open and close.

"I just now realized how sick I've been of

that hospital food!" she called to Marta. "Hey, I've got an idea! Why don't you call and order a pizza!"

There was no reply. "Marta, did you hear me?" she called again after a moment.

"You don't like pizza. Neither one of us does." Marta's voice came drifting into the living room.

The words struck Alicia like a drenching of cold water. It was impossible to describe how strange it felt to be told what sort of food you liked — or didn't like.

"Well — my stomach doesn't remember that I don't like it. Let's give it a try," Alicia said defiantly. She went back to examining the contents of the room.

There was a table crowded with pictures. She picked one up, and saw the faces of a worried-looking middle-aged couple. There was another framed portrait of them, and another one with a child who was unmistakably Marta.

They must be Mom and Dad, she thought, wishing she felt a glimmer of recognition. Painfully, she limped over to the mantel, where there were more pictures. She picked them up one after the other, trying to connect with her past.

"You don't like pizza," she heard Marta say, so close behind her that she jumped, and turned around.

Marta was holding a carving knife, the blade glinting in the stream of sunlight that filtered through the blinds.

"I think it's probably better if you try and do everything as much the way you used to do it as possible, don't you?" She saw Alicia staring at the knife, and lowered it.

"Take it easy. I was just going to make you a liverwurst sandwich. It's your favorite."

Mentally, Alicia searched the recipe file in her mind. Sandwiches. Liverwurst. Liverwurst. *Liverwurst.*

"Liverwurst?" She laughed nervously. "Isn't that an awfully big knife to cut liverwurst? Anyway, I don't think I like that."

Marta tilted her head to one side. "How can you say that, Alicia? You know you don't remember." She put one hand on her hip. "Trust me. It's your favorite." Her tone carried a finality that allowed no more argument. "I'll have it for you in a second." She began to walk back to the kitchen.

"Can't I help?"

"No," Marta said firmly, without turning around. "I'm going to take care of you until you get better. That's what sisters are for."

Feeling a little frustrated, Alicia watched her go. "I can make my own lunch, Mommy," she felt like saying. Marta had insisted on doing all the packing before they left the hospital, too. Alicia didn't like the way Marta had just taken over.

As soon as the thoughts had voiced themselves in her mind, though, she felt guilty. Marta was doing her best to help, and yet she wasn't feeling very grateful.

I'll let her do everything for a while if that's what she wants. After all, she's been very nice, and she's trying so hard.

Once again, Alicia went back to examining the pictures. There was Marta at around age six, playing in the snow.

What was I doing that day? she wondered. Will I ever remember?

Marta appeared as silently as before. Alicia didn't know she was there until she spoke. "Sandwich is ready. C'mon."

"Go ahead. I'll be in in a minute. I just want to look at these photographs a little longer."

Marta crossed her arms and spoke as if addressing a difficult child. "Now Alicia, you need to keep your strength up if you're going to get better. You can look at the photos later."

Alicia felt a prickle of irritation. She's only trying to help, she reminded herself. "All right."

Ever so slowly, so as to keep the pain in her leg to a minimum, Alicia followed Marta to the kitchen.

Two glasses of milk and two identical sandwiches were on the table.

"You're *sure* I like liverwurst?" Alicia asked in disbelief as she eyed the sandwich.

"It's your favorite," Marta told her again, smiling encouragingly.

Alicia sat down. With resignation, she took a bite of her sandwich. It was every bit as bad as she'd imagined it would be. She swallowed the bite with difficulty and drank several long gulps of milk.

Across the table, Marta was eating hungrily. She barely paused between bites. It looks as if *she's* the liverwurst lover, Alicia thought. Then the sight of Marta's canvas purse on the kitchen counter made her think of something.

"Marta, could I have a look at my pocketbook, or whatever sort of bag I had? Looking at my ID and the other stuff inside might help me remember something. Even just seeing the bag might help."

Across the table, Marta was already shaking

her head before Alicia finished speaking. She swallowed, and then took a drink of milk. "Sorry. I'm afraid they never found your bag. It was lost in the accident." She spoke quickly, hardly raising her eyes to Alicia's face. Then she went back to eating her sandwich.

"That's too bad," Alicia said softly. Then another thought occurred to her. "Well — maybe I'll remember some faces when I go back to school. I must have an awful lot to catch up on. It's kind of scary to think about how much work I must have missed."

Marta swallowed the last bite of her sandwich before replying.

"Alicia." She smiled and shook her head. "You can't possibly think of going back to school in your condition. Why, you've missed months of work, and you still have a lot of recovering to do."

Marta carried her dish to the sink and began washing it. "I've already discussed everything with the principal of your school. You'll start back next year. It's what everyone thinks is best." She turned and grinned at Alicia in a strangely maternal fashion.

Once again, Alicia felt a bewildering combination of resentment at being treated like a child and guilt *because Marta was only trying to help*. "I'm sorry," she said after a moment. "I didn't realize how tired I was. I think I have to lie down." She suddenly realized what had been intended as an excuse to get away from Marta's hovering presence — and get out of eating that awful sandwich — was really quite true.

Marta looked at her with a pinched expression. "What's wrong with your sandwich? You haven't touched it."

"Nothing's wrong with it," Alicia said hurriedly. "It's great. I'm just so tired. . . ."

After a moment Marta's expression cleared. "That's too bad. I was hoping we'd have time to talk. I'll take you upstairs to your room."

"I could just take a nap on the couch." Alicia thought of the pain her ankle would feel if she had to climb stairs.

"No," Marta said in a no-nonsense voice. "You belong in your room."

"All right," Alicia said. She was too tired to argue. Already she realized that Marta's mind was not easily changed once she'd decided on something.

"By the way," she said, as she got up from her chair. "Did I get along with our parents?"

"Oh, wonderfully," Marta said with a smile. "Everything was always just wonderful." She took Alicia's arm and helped her to her feet. "Come on. I'll take you to your room now."

The trip upstairs was slow and painful. Alicia had to lean heavily on Marta's arm. When she finally got to her room she collapsed on the bed with hardly a look at her surroundings. She was surprised and thankful that Marta left her alone and didn't insist that she change into pajamas.

As she drifted off to sleep, a vague, unformed worry that had been hovering around the edges of her mind suddenly sharpened to crystal clarity. If she hadn't been so tired, it would have kept her awake.

Marta said she and her parents got along well. In fact, everything was *perfect*. Why was it, then, that in all of the dozens of family pictures that crowded the tables and mantel, there had been none of her?

Chapter 7

Alicia opened her eyes. She was still caught between waking and sleeping — still half in a dream.

She wanted to stay inside the dream. When it began, the wind was rushing past her. She was rocketing down a road at night on a motorcycle, her arms wrapped around the waist of the boy who was driving it.

Then the dream had changed. She was in a room full of people, dancing with the same boy who had been on the motorcycle. She hadn't been able to see his face then, but still she knew it was he. The music was *soooooo* loud!

Her short, black skirt flared around her legs as she danced. She gazed deep into the eyes of the boy with the dark hair. His eyes were dark black pools that she got lost in as he danced closer . . . and closer. Then his arms were around her, pulling her close, and he lowered his mouth to hers. . . .

As she felt their lips touch, the dream began to spin away from her. As hard as she tried to hold on to it, still it slipped away, plummeting into nothingness, lost to her as she emerged through the dark cloud of sleep, and then awakened.

Her mind spun crazily. Where am I? The question shouted inside her head, echoing. Then she remembered she had been in a hospital, and now she was at home, in her own room.

She lay still for a moment until the pounding of her heart slowed. Out the window she could see that the first fingers of twilight were just beginning to reach across the sky. She must have just dozed off for a few hours.

She sat up slowly, and gently lowered her legs to the floor. Her hands felt her sore ankle. It was swollen. Well, no wonder, she thought. She'd done a lot more walking than she'd been doing in her hospital bed. And then Marta had insisted she walk up the stairs.

She inched over to the door to turn on the light. She remembered that light switches were always near the door. The room was flooded with light.

There's hardly any furniture in here, Alicia thought as she examined her surroundings.

Against one wall was a small, square desk with a metal lamp. In front of it was a straight-backed wooden chair.

A dresser with a mirror over it stood against another wall. It was plain, made of some sort of wood. Alicia ran her hand over it. I think it's pine, she said to herself, and immediately wondered why she thought she knew what pine looked like if she knew nothing about her own life.

Dr. Kellogg had explained about things like that in the hospital. Even though she had amnesia about everything personal, she might remember all sorts of other things — who the president was, how to make seafood gumbo, how to use a microwave, and what pine was. There was just no sense to it, Alicia thought.

She decided that her room was less creepy than the rest of the house. It didn't even look as if it *belonged* in the house. Although evidently I'm not a very imaginative decorator, she thought.

She began to notice some strange little details about the room. For one thing, there were no pictures or posters of any kind on the walls. In contrast to the living room, her room had no knickknacks, nor were there any vases or baskets of any kind.

There isn't even a CD player or radio. That's weird, she thought, looking around in surprise. And no television set. You'd certainly never know this was a teenager's room. In fact, you wouldn't know much about the person whose room this was at all.

The only impression you'd get is that this room belonged to someone with absolutely no imagination, whispered a little voice inside her head. No wonder I don't remember anything, she thought. There doesn't seem to have been much to remember. A feeling that was a mixture of uneasiness and disappointment stirred inside her.

Sighing, she opened her closet. I hope my clothes aren't as bland as everything else in my life, she prayed.

In the closet there were a couple of dresses, a jumper, some shirts, and skirts. Alicia removed a skirt and held it in front of her. It was straight and gray, the length neither very long nor very short. *Blah*, she thought, hanging it back in the closet.

An examination of the other items in the closet revealed no more encouraging results. Everything there was plain, dull, and drab.

The mixture of unease and disappointment grew stronger.

"Let's try the dresser," she whispered aloud. "Maybe that's where I keep all my really wild stuff." She pulled open the bottom drawer and found herself staring at a gray sweatshirt.

I was afraid this was what I'd find, she thought, shuffling through the contents of the drawer. Then she tried the middle drawer, and the top, all with uninspiring results.

By the time Alicia slid the last drawer closed, she was feeling disgusted and dejected. There's nothing with any personality or style whatsoever here, she thought, plopping down on the bed. I hardly know anything about myself, and all I want to do is change!

She glanced at the leather bracelet on her wrist. I like *this*, she thought. It's a whole different style from the clothes. It's hard to believe I chose them both.

After a moment she got up and limped over to the desk. The contents yielded even less information than the dresser had. All of the desk drawers were empty. There wasn't so much as a pencil or a single sheet of paper.

"Weird." Alicia whispered it over and over again as she gazed around the room, the thought sinking in that this was supposed to

be the room she had lived in all her life — and yet there was not one personal item — no photos, no letters, no jewelry, or perfume, or cosmetics. She looked down and saw her hands were shaking.

At first the room had seemed less creepy than the rest of the house. Now she thought it was just creepy in a different way. The skin on Alicia's neck started to pucker. Something was wrong here. *Dead wrong.*

She went to the closet and opened the door. Once again, she examined the clothes.

They may have been drab, but they certainly looked *new*. She picked up the sleeve of a sweater. Then she noticed the store tag was still attached. The tag was still attached to the blouse next to it, too.

Quickly, she rifled through every item in the closet. Every one had a tag attached.

Growing more and more fearful, Alicia pulled out the top bureau drawer and dumped everything on the bed. She picked up a pair of underpants. There were tags on those, too, and on all of the rest of the underwear.

Alicia sat down on the bed amidst the contents of the spilled drawer. Thoughts whirled in her head.

Her bag had been lost in the accident. She

had no identification whatsoever.

She didn't remember this house, or this room. She couldn't remember the clothes, because none of them had belonged to her — they were all new. There were no photographs of her. There was absolutely nothing to indicate that she had ever lived here at all.

And she didn't remember her sister.

Chapter 8

"Marta!"

Alicia looked up and saw her standing in the doorway, still as a statue, with a stonelike expression on her face. Alicia hadn't heard her footsteps, but she'd suddenly had the sensation of being watched . . . she'd *felt* her presence as surely as if Marta had reached out and touched her. Sure enough, when she'd looked up from the pile of clothing on her bed, there was Marta.

How long has she been standing there? Alice wondered. Marta was leaning against the door frame with the relaxed attitude of someone who has made herself comfortable. From the way she looked, Alicia imagined she hadn't just arrived, but had been there a while, watching as drawer after drawer was emptied.

"Alicia, what in the world have you been

doing? Why are the clothes scattered all over the bed?" Marta's eyes glittered with a hard, brittle brightness.

Alicia let her gaze wander over Marta's face, examining it once again for resemblance between them. There isn't any, she decided.

Our hair is different, and so is the color of our eyes. Even our posture is different. We don't walk the same, or talk the same.

"Alicia, answer me." Now Marta looked innocently perplexed.

"I'd rather ask some questions of my own." Alicia picked up a cotton shirt and held it up. "Every piece of clothing in this room has a department store tag on it. It's all new. There's nothing that *belonged* to me."

Marta's glance darted back and forth before she answered. "Don't be silly. The clothes are all yours. What do you mean there's nothing that belonged to you?" Her brows knitted, giving her a confused expression.

Alicia threw the shirt down on the bed. "There's nothing that I've worn before." She jumped to her feet, getting a slash of pain in return for forgetting her injured ankle.

"Oh, goodness." Marta hurried toward her.

Alicia held her hand up. "Stay away. I'll be all right in a minute."

When the pain had subsided to a degree where she could speak again, Alicia gestured at the room. "It isn't just the clothes. *Everything* in here looks new. There's nothing personal of mine."

The confusion cleared from Marta's face, and she smiled broadly. "But there's a *perfect* explanation. One day you decided you wanted everything changed — your clothes, your room — everything." Marta shook her head and gave a little chuckle.

"Well, when you decide you want something done, you go ahead and do it. You took all your clothes and furniture to the Salvation Army store in town. Whatever was left, you threw away."

Alicia's mouth dropped open. "Just like that? That's incredible. What did Mom and Dad do?"

Marta laughed again, the sound issuing from her lips in a combination of mirth and hiccups. "What could they do? You needed clothes and furniture. Besides, you'd saved up a lot of money from baby-sitting and doing odd jobs, so you paid for a lot of this yourself."

Alicia sat down on the bed, looking at the plain furniture and thinking about the drab clothes in the closet. She was stunned that she had actually picked everything out. It seemed impossible.

She remembered the bracelet. "Look at this, Marta." She held up her wrist. "It's so different from the clothes. It's a whole different style. It seems so weird that I chose this and I chose those clothes."

Marta looked at her blankly for a moment. Then a look of understanding crossed her face. "I know what you mean. You bought that bracelet from a little old man at a crafts fair because you felt sorry for him. He practically begged you to buy it."

"Oh," Alicia said softly. The whole thing was so incredible. "I can't believe I spent money for a whole new wardrobe," she said. "Wasn't I saving for college, Marta?"

Now Marta looked serious. "Well — no. You didn't want to go to college, because you'd have to leave home. You were planning to get a job here in town."

"Oh," Alicia said in a small voice. "I certainly wasn't very ambitious, was I?"

"Well, why in the world would you want to do something that would mean you had to leave home?"

Alicia looked up and saw that Marta's

expression had darkened as if a shadow from within had fallen across her face. "We were such a close family. Especially you and me," said Marta. *"Sisters should stick together."*

Alicia ran a hand through her hair. She felt uncomfortable with this explanation. It just didn't add up somehow.

She turned to Marta, whose face was frozen in a look of solid disapproval. "If we were such a close family, why aren't there any pictures of me in the house? There are loads of photographs here, but I'm not in a single one."

Marta's body stiffened. She walked to the window, and with her back to Alicia, she said quietly, "You had a little feud with Mom and Dad about six months ago. You took all the pictures of yourself that were in the house and burned them."

"Burned them! Why?"

After a moment, Marta turned to Alicia. "It wasn't a big deal at all. It was just one of those teenage things." She gave a little shrug. "We were all very upset, Mom and Dad and I. You'd never done anything like that before. We couldn't imagine what got into you."

"There's nothing?"

"Nothing."

Alicia got to her feet carefully this time. She

felt like running — running to see if she recognized anything as she ran past it.

But, of course, she couldn't run. It hurt just to walk.

"I'd just like to be alone for a while, please, Marta. I want to think some things over."

"Well . . . all right," Marta said, slowly. She walked over to the bed and began folding the clothes. "Gosh darn it! You've made a big mess. I'll just put these away for you first."

"Marta, I'll do it! Just leave me alone!" Alicia was surprised at her own outburst. But she was more surprised at the fury in Marta's voice when she answered.

"You never appreciated anything I did for you!" Marta said, her face twisted in a grimace of rage. Her big hands clenched and unclenched themselves at her sides. For a fleeting instant, Alicia thought she might walk over and strike her. Then Marta stormed from the room, slamming the door behind her.

When she was gone, Alicia limped to the single chair in the room and sat down. She felt weak, as if the encounter with Marta had drained away her energy. I've got to get better, and stronger, she thought, resting her head in her hands.

There's something going on here that Marta

isn't telling me. Suddenly getting rid of all of one's clothing and furniture isn't the act of a sensible person. It doesn't fit with the mild-mannered me that Marta described.

Nor did burning photographs sound like something that "was no big deal," especially if everything about family life was as hunky-dory as Marta said.

Hunky-dory, Alicia repeated to herself. That sounded like something Marta might say. She had a lot of those funny little words that sounded, well — goofy. Like *oopsie daisy* and *gosh darn it,* and *fiddle-faddle.*

The skin on the back of her neck prickled. *Everything* about Marta was just a little out of step — the way she didn't laugh until Alicia did and then joined in with that hiccuping sound, the way her expressions changed from moment to moment. Being around Marta was like watching a dancer who couldn't keep the beat.

Alicia raised her head and looked around at the sparsely furnished room. Marta wasn't the only part of the picture that was offbeat. There was something wrong about all of this.

A feeling of vague foreboding formed itself into a pool of nausea in Alicia's stomach. Her homecoming wasn't a happy event, after all. She didn't want to listen to the voice that was whispering inside her head, but she couldn't get away from it.

You're in a lot of trouble.

Chapter 9

Less than an hour had passed since Marta had stormed out of Alicia's room when she breezed back in without knocking. Alicia was about to tell her not to do that again, but the words vanished as soon as she saw Marta's face.

Gone were all traces of the twisted rage. Her face was lit up with smiles.

She was holding something behind her back. "I have a surprise for you," she said. Her eyes twinkled. "Do you want to know what it is?"

"Sure." Alicia hoped she didn't look as astonished as she felt. The quick transformation in Marta's disposition was so eerily fascinating, she had to stop herself from gaping.

Keeping whatever it was hidden behind her, Marta stepped closer. The smile slipped from her face and she looked solemn.

"Before I show you the surprise, I have to

say something." Marta drew herself up stiff and straight. "You know, Alicia. It's not right for sisters to fight. We never fought before."

Alicia gave herself a little shake. "You can't be serious, Marta. You're trying to tell me that we never had a single fight growing up? It's impossible."

"Why don't you believe me? It's *true*," Marta said in a faltering voice. Now her lip quivered slightly. Is she really going to *cry*? Alicia wondered.

Before she could say anything, Marta was beaming again. She held out her "surprise."

"Look what I found, Alicia! I went searching for it as soon as I left your room. When I got my hands on it, I was so excited I couldn't wait to show you!"

Marta held out a large brown book with a cracked leather cover. "It's an old photograph album from when we were kids. I remembered it was up in the attic, but I wasn't sure if you'd gone and burned the pictures in here with the rest of them. Golly day! It's lucky you forgot!" She pressed the album into Alicia's hands. "Go on and take it. Maybe you'll remember how well we got along when you look at these pictures. Maybe then you'll believe we never fought."

Wordlessly, Alicia took the album over to her desk and sat down. Her hands trembled as she opened it.

There, on the first page, was a photograph of her and Marta sitting in a sandbox, looking at each other and laughing. They were about ages four and seven.

In another photograph, Marta was pushing Alicia on a swing. And in another, they were eating ice-cream cones.

Alicia was caught up in a wave of emotion. Here was the life that she couldn't remember.

She looked up from the album, and saw that Marta had already folded many of the clothes on the bed and was picking up the remaining ones quickly, one after the other, all the time shaking her head and mumbling, "What a mess!"

Alicia felt a twinge of irritation, but it passed quickly. She was too happy about seeing the pictures to let anything bother her. Now her fears about Marta seemed incredibly silly. Marta was a little quirky, that's all. She'd certainly done her best to look after her.

Alicia turned to the next page in the album. There were Alicia and Marta riding ponies. She turned page after page, all full of pictures of the two of them, always smiling or laughing. But she remembered nothing.

When she'd looked at the last page of photographs, Alicia closed the album and put it down on the desk. Marta had finished putting everything away and was just standing there.

"Well, Alicia? Any memories?"

Alicia shook her head. "Nope. But I still liked looking at the photos. And you're right — it looks like we got along awfully well."

A smile lit up Marta's face.

"I'll look at the pictures some more, and sooner or later the memories will come. Thanks for putting the clothes away, but you really don't have to do everything for me."

Marta made a dismissive gesture with her hand. "Nonsense. I'm happy to help you. That's what sisters are for. And now I'm going to go downstairs and make you a nice cup of hot cocoa."

"Thanks, Marta, but I don't want any right now."

Marta's smile disappeared for an instant, but then reappeared. "You just don't remember how much you enjoyed it when we had cocoa together. It will only be a minute."

Alicia watched her go. I hope that when the

novelty wears off Marta will stop hovering over me, she prayed.

Her hand brushed the cracked leather cover of the album. She opened it again and began thumbing through the pages.

How strange to know that I'm looking at pictures of Marta and me, and not remember anything about the times when the photographs were taken, she thought.

But then something made her pause and stare at a picture of her standing with Marta in front of a Ferris wheel. Like far-off music, a memory stirred, distant at first, then sweeping over her with a rush of sound, sights, and the smells of popcorn, hot dogs, and cotton candy.

Alicia's heart pounded. "I was there," she whispered, looking at the picture. The lights and whirl of activity painted themselves in broad strokes across her mind, bolder and bolder.

She remembered that she and Marta had gone on ride after ride. Then they had both eaten huge clouds of pink cotton candy.

Alicia hugged the worn photo album to her chest. I should be overjoyed about remembering anything at all, but I'm not. Why?

She answered herself. The fear hadn't gone

away. She'd seen pictures from her past, and even remembered something, but she was still filled with anxiety. If anything, it had gotten worse, because now she didn't have a cause for it.

Before she'd thought her fear had something to do with Marta. Now that seemed silly. She wasn't afraid of Marta anymore. She was just *afraid*.

From some dark chamber inside her mind, she recalled Dr. Kellogg's words. Sometimes amnesia means there's something you're too afraid to remember.

Chapter 10

Alicia dreamed she was running, running, down the dark tunnel again, while the accusing dark stranger with the blazing eyes pursued her. But this time, she made it out of the tunnel.

It ended abruptly. Suddenly, her gray frame house loomed before her. Without understanding how she got there, she found herself on the porch. Then the door opened.

"Welcome."

Nurse Tra-la-la stood before her. She looked different from before. This time her eyes were ringed with smudges of eye shadow, the lashes clumped together with thick mascara. On her cheeks were two bright, hectic spots of red, and her mouth was a crimson slash across her face.

"I'm so glad you're home, Alicia, dear. I have a surprise for you."

She held a jacket out toward Alicia. "Go on, dear. Put it on. It was made for you."

Alicia looked at the jacket. There was something strange about it. Then she understood what was wrong. *It was a straitjacket.* And then (but it was impossible!) she saw that Nurse Tra-la-la was wearing a straitjacket, too.

Alicia started to scream — or at least she tried. When she opened her mouth, no sound came out.

She was jerked from the dream and suddenly sat up in bed awake in the darkened room. Her heart was pounding, and her mouth was still open in the silent scream.

After a moment she was calm enough to glance at the glowing fluorescent numbers on the face of the clock at her bedside. Three-thirty A.M. The same time she'd awakened for the past — oh, how many nights? She slumped back against the pillows.

One day had blended into the next. She'd been home nearly a week now, and after the flash of recognition she'd had looking at the picture of the carnival, she'd had no more memories. And the fear had persisted. Sometimes she was nearly able to forget it, but always it hovered at the edges of her mind. Sooner or later it returned full force.

She'd spoken to Marta about the bad dreams and the fear. Marta had pooh-poohed her worries. In fact, that's exactly what she had said, "Oh, pooh-pooh — there's nothing for you to be afraid of. You feel scared because you can't remember who you are. As soon as you remember what a happy life you had here, and get back to it, the fear will go away. So will the bad dreams."

It sounded so sensible. But as hard as she tried to believe it, it didn't work. Fear was her constant companion by day, and followed her into her dreams.

Night after night began with variations of the same nightmare that started with her running from someone in a tunnel. The only dreams that didn't terrify her were the ones she had about dancing with the dark-haired boy and riding behind him on his motorcycle.

She'd asked Marta about the dark-haired boy in her dreams. Marta had told her there had been no such boy in real life.

Alicia chuckled to herself in the dark. Riding a motorcycle and dancing wildly with a handsome boy certainly didn't mesh with the Alicia she'd been told about. That girl would rather do a crossword puzzle.

But the things she did in the dream seemed exciting and fun, and so real. After a while, Alicia drifted back into a restless sleep, yearning for the dark-haired boy.

She awakened to the sound of Marta's voice. Marta wasn't in the same room with her — she was somewhere else in the house. And she wasn't talking to anyone who was here, that much was certain, because the only voice Alicia heard was Marta's. She was talking on the telephone.

Funny — Alicia realized she hadn't heard the telephone ring since she'd been here. I guess I was just too out of it to notice, she thought. She strained her ears to hear what Marta was saying.

"Tired . . . No, I don't think so. . . . too soon. . . . Alicia can't. . . . She's visiting . . . relatives."

The last statement went through Alicia like a shock. Why would Marta tell someone she was visiting relatives? Maybe it was one of her friends!

She struggled to sit up. But before she could even get her feet on the floor, she heard Marta saying, "I'm sorry. I really can't talk any longer. I'm late for work."

There was the sound of the telephone receiver being replaced in its cradle; the sound of Marta's quick steps; the sounds of the door opening and then shutting with a soft *click*.

Alicia dropped back against the pillows. She turned her head to look at the time — ten o'clock. No wonder Marta didn't wake me up, she thought. She must be *very* late.

Marta woke her up before seven every morning and made her a big breakfast. No matter how many times Marta told her she loved to eat a big breakfast, she always dreaded the meal. I guess my appetite has lost its memory, too, she'd said to Marta one morning. Marta hadn't laughed.

Alicia turned over in bed and noticed that the movement caused no twinge of pain in her ankle. It was getting better. She decided she was ready to do some more walking.

She'd been staying off it as much as possible since the first day she'd been home. When Marta saw how swollen her ankle had become, she'd said she was sorry for insisting that Alicia walk upstairs to her room. She'd brought up all her meals and waited on her hand and foot.

At first Alicia had been so exhausted and in

pain she was actually grateful. But as she started to feel better, Marta's hovering became more and more annoying. Yesterday she'd gotten so restless she'd wanted to go downstairs, but Marta talked her out of it.

Well, she won't talk me out of it today, Alicia said to herself. But first she decided to take advantage of Marta's absence and sleep late. She rolled over and was sound asleep in seconds.

When Alicia awoke again, it was nearly three in the afternoon. She yawned and stretched happily. She felt better than she had since she'd gotten home.

Her ankle hardly hurt at all. When she examined it she could see that the swelling was almost gone.

Moments later, Alicia stood in front of the bathroom mirror. You're looking better now, too, she told herself as she smiled at her reflection. Her eyes had lost the dark circles, and the exhausted, drawn look was gone from her face.

As Alicia brushed her teeth, she pondered the phone conversation. Who was it? she wondered. And why did Marta tell them I've gone to visit relatives?

Alicia washed her face and finished with several splashes of cold water. She knew the reason Marta would give her. Marta always did what she thought was best for her sister. That's what she always said.

Back in her room, Alicia faced the discouraging task of finding something to wear. She shifted the hangers this way and that, her frown growing bigger by the minute as she looked at each item. They all seemed so nerdy — so lacking in any kind of style.

Finally she chose a gray sweatshirt and a pair of black slacks. There isn't even a pair of jeans here, Alicia thought, incredulously. I've simply got to get some decent clothes.

Marta will just tell me a shopping trip is too stressful for me, she thought with impatience. Then she had an idea. Marta's always saying *sisters have to stick together.* I'll tell her we'll make it a "sisters" event. Sisters shopping together. A smile spread over her face. Once Marta saw she could handle shopping, maybe she'd stop smothering her so much. I certainly hope so, Alicia said to herself. Now where was that telephone?

An hour later she was no closer to finding it. It doesn't make sense, she said to herself. If I didn't know better, I'd think we didn't have one.

Finally, on her third examination of the living room, she found it. It was tucked under a stool in a corner with the wire wrapped around it.

I guess Marta didn't want the ringing phone to bother me, Alicia thought.

In moments she located the jack and plugged the phone in. It was nice to hear a dial tone again. She hadn't heard one in a long time.

Alicia held the receiver in her hand. *Now what?* she wondered. She hadn't thought this far.

Who am I going to call? She didn't know a single number . . . or name.

Refusing to let her enthusiasm be dampened, Alicia decided to order a pizza. She'd been trying to talk Marta into getting one for days, with no success.

Now, how to find the pizzeria? They passed one on the way here . . . what was the name? Ken's! Ken's Pizza Palace.

"Yes!" Alicia murmured to the empty house.

She had just started to dial when she heard Marta's key in the door. Before she had a chance to speak, Marta looked at her holding the telephone receiver and her eyes widened. "Alicia, what in the world are you doing?" Marta took three giant steps and grabbed the phone from her hand.

Stunned, Alicia could only say, "I — I was just going to make a call."

In a single swift motion, Marta pulled the telephone wire from the jack. Looking at Alicia, she said, in a tone one would use to admonish a small child, "Sorry. No phone calls."

Chapter 11

Paralyzed with shock, Alicia could only watch as Marta took the telephone receiver from her hand and replaced it in its cradle. Then she wrapped the cord around the telephone several times.

"I'm going to put this away, do you understand?" Marta's face was flushed and her eyes glittered with intensity.

Alicia nodded numbly.

"Now, you wait right here."

Marta disappeared upstairs while Alicia, too stunned to move, did as she was told. She heard Marta moving about upstairs. She must be putting the phone in her own room, Alicia thought.

Suddenly, her shock subsided and was replaced by a burst of anger. Who does Marta think she is to speak to me like that? Alicia set her mouth into a thin line.

Here I stand doing what she told me to do, like a bad child. Well, I've had enough.

Squaring her shoulders, she went out to the kitchen. She was going to have a snack before dinner. Not because she was hungry, but because she knew Marta wouldn't like it.

By the time she heard Marta's footsteps on the stairs, Alicia was seated at the kitchen table munching on chocolate chip cookies.

"Alicia? Where are you?"

She felt a twinge of satisfaction when she heard the worry in Marta's voice. It was worry that gave it that high-pitched squeak at the end.

"Alicia? *Alicia?*" The squeak became more pronounced. Alicia could hear Marta's footsteps getting closer and sat quietly.

"*Alicia! Ali* — Oh!" Marta stood still suddenly as she saw Alicia sitting calmly at the kitchen table. "There you are. I told you to stay right where you were. Why didn't you answer me?" She faced Alicia with a stonelike stare.

Alicia stared back at her in silence.

Marta's eyes wavered. The stony stare began to slip. Gradually, it was replaced by a look of uncertainty.

"I'm sorry I got so upset." Marta slowly crossed over to the kitchen table. After a moment's hesitancy, she sat down. She glanced at the cookies briefly, but must have thought it wise not to comment.

"Don't ever order me around again. Why don't you want me to talk on the phone?" Alicia demanded. "I heard you this morning, telling someone I'd gone away. Why did you do that?"

"Alicia, please don't be angry. I was just so worried about you," Marta said, staring into Alicia's eyes.

"That's why you don't want me to talk to anyone? It doesn't make sense," Alicia snapped.

"Well, the doctors told me that if you were going to remember anything, you should be quiet — not too much stress, not too much at once. They said we should just do things together at home the way we used to. They said it was too soon to talk to other people. We should wait until you were more yourself again." Marta's voice took on an indignant edge. "I feel responsible for you. I'm sorry that you don't understand that what I'm doing is for your own good."

Alicia sighed.

"I know you're trying to do what's best for me, Marta. Shouldn't I at least start seeing a therapist to talk about what might have caused the amnesia? The doctor thought it might not be physical, but something that happened that I don't want to remember."

"Phooey! That's ridiculous!" Marta said emphatically. "Maybe she thought that at one time, but now they know that's not true. It's all because of the accident." She wiped her eyes with the back of her hand and spoke more quietly. "The doctor says it's too soon to start therapy, and you should just stay at home for a while. Maybe then you'll remember on your own, and you won't need the therapy at all." Marta looked at Alicia as if she were trying to reason with a small child.

Alicia felt a rippling of uneasiness mingled with frustration. "It doesn't make sense to stay home alone and not talk to anyone!"

Marta faced her with an icy stare. "Stay home alone and not talk to anyone," she echoed. "Who am I . . . nobody?"

"That's not what I meant!" Alicia said, feeling more and more flustered. She looked down at the tabletop and took a long, deep breath. Then she looked back at Marta. "I can't help feeling that you're keeping something from me. It's true, isn't it?"

Marta rolled her eyes. "For heaven's sake, Alicia, listen to yourself. You're the one who isn't making sense. I've told you what the doctors said you should do, that's all."

Alicia stood up suddenly. "I don't care. I want to talk to my friends."

Marta looked toward the window. "Well, I can't help you. I don't know the names of any of your friends. You never mentioned any. Besides, they aren't very good friends, anyway. None of them has come by to visit you since you've been home. If I were you, I'd say good riddance to bad company."

"Well, they won't know I'm here if you lie to them on the phone the way you did this morning," Alicia retorted.

Marta's eyes opened wide. "The person I was talking to was no friend of yours, it was . . ." She let her voice trail off. "It wasn't anyone important, Alicia. Please trust me."

Her voice took on a hurt tone. "We were always so close, but now it doesn't seem that you feel that way. I'm only trying to do my best. I miss the way we used to be." She slumped dejectedly in her chair.

Alicia could feel the guilt crowding in once more.

"There must be a way to find out the names of my friends. I think it would help me to talk to them, no matter what the doctor says." She tried to put more certainty into her voice. "After all, even a doctor can make a mistake."

Then she had an idea. "I know! I'll call the school. I can find out the names of my teachers. They'll know who I was friendly with."

Marta looked at her with an expression of long-suffering patience. She sighed, a sound that said *here we go again* more clearly than any words could.

"Why would you want to talk to people you don't remember?"

"But — "

"It would only upset you. Besides — do you want people to look at you as an oddity? To ask how it feels to forget who you are? Maybe even think you're . . . crazy?"

Alicia felt herself floundering in the face of Marta's logic. Then Marta gave her such a slyly knowing smile they both knew that once again, Alicia had lost and Marta had won.

"Let's not fight," Marta said, laying a hand on Alicia's shoulder. "Sisters have to stick together."

Chapter 12

Three days had passed since the telephone incident. The telephone never reappeared. Marta kept it hidden in her room. At least, Alicia was pretty sure that's where it was, especially since she'd tried the door several times, and it was always locked.

She hadn't heard Marta talking on the phone again. She never heard it ringing, either.

Every day she hoped for new memories, but none came. Now Dr. Kellogg's words, *sometimes amnesia means there's something you're afraid to remember,* kept appearing and reappearing in her mind.

Again she had asked Marta if she was keeping something from her. Marta had insisted she wasn't. "It's just the amnesia that makes you feel fearful," she told her once more. "The doctors said it's a common side effect."

Marta had sounded so certain that Alicia had almost been able to make herself believe it. For a few moments the fear had gone away. But the doubt came back. So did the fear.

Meanwhile, Marta continued to do everything possible for her. She woke Alicia at seven each morning and made a big breakfast before going to work. Now, however, Alicia was able to go downstairs and sit at the kitchen table.

Breakfast was a particularly trying time for Alicia. If she started to butter a piece of toast, Marta took it from her and buttered it. If she started to spoon sugar into her tea, Marta would take the spoon from her and add it herself. Alicia felt smothered by her attentions. Marta just didn't understand that. "I'm here to take care of you. That's what sisters are for," she would say.

One morning Alicia had protested she was strong enough to get her own breakfast.

"Isn't what I'm doing good enough for you?" Marta had blurted out. After that, Alicia kept silent.

Now that she was spending time downstairs, she was surprised to find there was no television set in the house. There wasn't even a radio.

"Our parents had something against that

sort of thing," Marta had told her. "They thought it was better to read."

But Alicia noticed Marta didn't do much reading. In fact, when she thought about it, she couldn't recall having ever seen her do *any* reading. She never brought a newspaper or magazine into the house.

"I'm too busy taking care of you to peruse newspapers and magazines," Marta said. "Besides, instead of thinking about watching television, and listening to the radio, and reading, it's better if you concentrate on doing things you used to do and getting your memory back."

So Alicia tried to do just that. Every day when Marta left for work she tried to rest and do the word games and crossword puzzles that Marta told her she liked.

When Marta came home from work she made dinner, and then she and Alicia would play some sort of game Marta picked out, or a jigsaw puzzle.

Alicia hoped some memory of enjoying the puzzles and games would return, but it didn't. In fact, she couldn't even imagine ever enjoying them. She didn't now, and she wasn't very good at them, either.

The three days that had passed were so

chock-full of boredom, they dragged by as if they were never ending. Alicia was growing restless, bored, and edgy.

That evening after dinner, she watched Marta reaching for a jigsaw puzzle on the bookshelf in the living room, and she felt her stomach tightening in knots. Oh, no, not again, she said silently. I can't face one more evening of puzzles and games.

"Can't we do something else?" she blurted out. The words just came out of her mouth as if on their own. She hardly realized she had said anything until she heard the words. But she knew that she'd made a mistake.

Marta's body stiffened suddenly. Slowly, she took the puzzle from the shelf and put it on the coffee table.

"I thought you enjoyed doing puzzles together," she said in a low voice. She stared at Alicia intently.

"Oh, I do, I do," Alicia said hurriedly. "Doing something else was just an idea. We can do the puzzle if you've got your heart set on it."

But it was too late to make amends. Alicia saw Marta was grinding her teeth, and she didn't like the look in her eyes.

"Just what is wrong with doing a jigsaw puzzle?" Marta reached up and gave her hair a tug.

Alicia spoke haltingly. "Well, nothing is wrong with it, Marta. Come on, forget what I said. We'll put it together."

"No, no. You don't like it. I can see that now," Marta said. She gave her hair another tug and walked toward Alicia.

"You used to enjoy putting puzzles together and playing games with your sister. But since you've come home this time, you don't."

She kept walking toward Alicia, until she stood right in front of her. "No matter how hard I try and try, you don't appreciate anything."

For a moment, Marta's eyes were glowing with rage. Then she gave a casual shrug and walked back to the coffee table. "So what, it's no skin off my nose," she said. She picked up the puzzle and removed the cover. Then, without warning, she heaved the puzzle against the wall. Pieces scattered everywhere, bouncing off furniture, landing all over the floor, tables, the couch.

Marta's fists were clenched at her sides. "If what I want to do isn't good enough for you, maybe your sister isn't good enough for you, either!"

Alicia could only stand there, too astounded to move or say a word, as Marta picked up a figurine from the table. It looked as if she was going to throw it, too. She drew her hand back and was about to let it fly, when at the last minute she caught herself.

Alicia could tell Marta was restraining herself with considerable effort. After holding the figurine motionless for several moments, she replaced it on the table. Then she stormed up the stairs. There was the sound of her bedroom door slamming.

Alicia felt weak, as if her knees would buckle under her. She sank down onto the couch.

The whole incident was a kind of blur in her mind. Marta's rage had erupted out of nowhere. And all over a jigsaw puzzle!

After a few minutes Alicia got up and started picking up puzzle pieces. What happened had seemed so strange. What in the world is the matter with Marta? she wondered.

Then she realized that Marta had been growing more and more moody lately. Sometimes she just sat and stared, and she'd had some fits of temper. Nothing, however, like tonight.

"Alicia!"

Startled, Alicia gasped. She hadn't heard

Marta come downstairs, and yet she was standing right beside her. Her fists were clenched at her sides.

"Don't you dare touch those puzzle pieces. You leave them right where they are!" Marta grabbed the box with a few pieces that had been collected and pulled it from Alicia's hands. She flung the pieces back on the floor.

"Leave them right where they are!" she said once more, and then marched upstairs again. The bedroom door slammed a second time, and there was an angry creak of springs as she flung herself on her bed.

Alicia stood in the empty living room with puzzle pieces strewn about and found herself trembling. She hoped Marta wouldn't come downstairs again and appear beside her out of nowhere. Because tonight Marta had really acted . . . crazy.

Chapter 13

The following morning, Marta didn't awaken Alicia. Instead she left bacon and eggs on a covered dish with a note on the kitchen table. The note said she was sorry about what happened last night, and also that she had to rush to work for a big meeting.

All of the puzzle pieces had been picked up, but Marta had left the dishes from last night's dinner, plus some more from that morning, in the sink. It wasn't like her at all.

Only then, Alicia realized that since the telephone incident, Marta hadn't been such a stickler for neatness. Her cleaning routine had slacked off, too. Alicia used to hear her bustling around as she lay in bed. Marta even ran the vacuum cleaner at all hours of the night. She was compulsive about cleaning . . . but not lately.

As Alicia sat down to her breakfast, she thought about how Marta had been taking care of her, plus having an important job. Perhaps Marta was overworked and tired, and that was the reason for her outburst the night before. She had too much to do and needed some help.

Yet whenever Alicia offered to help, Marta refused. Alicia decided she'd have to *show* Marta she could share the responsibility instead of asking her. And that's what led to her decision to go into town to stock up on some groceries they were running low on.

Growing more and more excited with the prospect of her adventure into town, Alicia threw down her napkin and got up from the table. She was so excited, in fact, that it was only as she was ready to head out the door that she remembered she didn't have any money. How would she buy things?

Automatically, her eyes flickered toward the cupboard where she knew Marta kept money in the glass jar behind the cups. Taking it wouldn't be like stealing, she reasoned. She'd be using it to buy something they both needed.

She crossed to the cupboard, pushed aside the cups and reached for the jar. After a brief moment's hesitation, she twisted the lid off, took out a five-dollar bill, and slipped it into the pocket of her slacks. She started to put the jar back, but hesitated.

There must be at least three hundred dollars in the jar, she thought. Enough to buy a lot more than a few groceries.

Alicia stared at the money. There was enough to buy a pair of jeans — and some makeup! Alicia realized how much she missed putting on lipstick. Marta never wore any.

Feeling a twinge of guilt, she took several bills and slipped them into her pocket. It's *our* money, after all, she argued silently. The groceries are for both of us, and if I get anything for myself, I'll pay back the money.

By the time Marta gets home, I'll be back. I'll do something for her . . . I'll make dinner! She'll be so relieved that she doesn't have to do everything herself anymore, she won't mind.

Alicia couldn't quite believe any of that, but she refused to worry about it. The idea of going into town was too tempting. The only problem was how to get there. Humming happily, she closed the front door and headed down the street.

As it turned out, getting to town wasn't very difficult after all. Alicia spotted the sign for

Ken's Pizza Palace right away. It wasn't much past the end of the block.

Soon she was pushing open the door and inhaling the fragrant aroma of the pies. It smells wonderful in here, she said to herself. Now we'll find out if Marta is right about my not liking pizza.

"A slice, please," she told the sullen-looking man behind the counter. "And a Coke."

As Alicia waited for her order, she looked around. Ken's had the rough yet cozy look of a place that had been around for quite a while.

The walls were painted dark green, and there were booths with high-backed seats along one wall. Square tables with red-checkered tablecloths stood on the tile floor.

As Alicia looked at the place, she thought she felt a spark of recognition. Expectantly, she waited for the memory to grow stronger. She looked from this part of the place to that, her eyes moving over the mirrors on the walls, the tables, chairs, even the cash register.

But instead of a memory that grew to a rush of crystal clarity, the spark simply vanished. False alarm, she said to herself.

"Here you go," the man behind the counter said, sliding over a slice of pizza and a drink on a tray.

"Thanks." Alicia paid him and picked up the tray. She started walking away, then stopped and turned around. "Do you remember me?" she asked.

The man was counting money into the register. He looked up sharply, his features etched with surprise and annoyance. "Huh?"

"I said, do you remember me?"

The man looked at Alicia as if she'd lost her mind. "Nah. I've never seen you before," he said gruffly.

Well *excuse me*, Alicia thought. She carried her food to a table in a corner near the window.

It was after lunch, but too early for school to let out. The place was empty. Alicia had her choice of tables. She picked one far from the counter and the cranky man behind it, and sat down.

Here goes, Alicia thought, biting into the slice of pizza. The crust was thin and crisp, the sauce tangy, and there was plenty of melted cheese.

Well, at least the guy sure knows how to cook, Alicia said to herself, eyeing the man behind the counter. *This is great.* She took bite after bite. I *love* pizza, she said to herself. How could Marta be so mistaken as to think I didn't?

Alicia toyed with her soda straw. Maybe Marta didn't know her as well as she thought. She thought I didn't like pizza, and I loved puzzles and games. Maybe she was mistaken about lots of things.

The bell over the door jingled, and a man entered. He was wearing a dark-blue denim jacket and had a long, thick scar on his face. His dark hair was peppered with gray, and he had piercing brown eyes.

The man ordered a soda and carried it to a table in the back of the restaurant. All the while, his gaze roamed all around the place. It was constantly shifting and often rested on her.

He certainly looks tough, Alicia thought. In fact, he looks like somebody who likes to cause trouble.

She got up and threw away her trash in the garbage can. She got directions to town from the man behind the counter and left. The whole time she talked to the counterman, she thought the man with the scar was staring at her, even though her back was to him. She was glad to be on her way.

The pizza man had told her that town wasn't far, just a mile or so straight down the road. Alicia walked along, noting that her ankle wasn't bothering her at all. She moved at a brisk pace and could see the low buildings of the town drawing near in no time.

Alicia sped up her pace. Every so often, she kept looking over her shoulder. It wasn't anything she heard or saw, but something she felt. Each time she looked, no one was there. Until the last time.

She had just reached the town when she turned to look over her shoulder once more. Then she saw the man with the scar on his face.

He was shuffling along, with his hands in his pockets, as if he was just taking an aimless stroll. But Alicia wasn't fooled by his pretense.

She knew he was following her.

Chapter 14

Her pulse quickening with fear, Alicia looked for a way to lose the scar-faced stranger on her trail. She wanted to run, but didn't dare, for fear that he'd run after her and grab her.

Ahead she saw the sign DAISY DRUGS. At least inside the drug store, there would be people, and maybe she could lose him in all the activity.

Daisy Drugs turned out to be a dream come true. Shoppers galore bustled through aisle after aisle of merchandise. Gigantic plastic daisies were everywhere, proclaiming Daisy Bargain Days.

Alicia hurried to the back of the store, trying her best to be inconspicuous. Why was the man following her? she wondered. Did he know her? She couldn't explain it, but she had a strong feeling he *did*, and that the relationship between them hadn't been a pleasant one. Was he somehow connected to whatever it was that was too scary to remember?

After several minutes of hiding behind a shampoo display topped with a big yellow daisy, Alicia grew bolder. She ventured out of her hiding place and began strolling through the aisles, her eyes darting here and there, searching for the man. But the man with the shifty brown eyes and the scar seemed to have vanished.

Alicia looked around at the people hurrying through the brightly lit aisles and felt foolish. Her fears suddenly seemed outlandish. He probably wasn't even following you, silly, she told herself. Maybe Marta's right — the amnesia is making you fearful. All your dark fears about the past and something that Marta is keeping from you are probably just your imagination, too.

Soon all thoughts of the scar-faced man were put out of her head in the excitement of all the new things to see.

Alicia bought a lipstick at the cosmetics counter, and then hurried outside in search of a store where she could buy a pair of jeans.

Her enthusiasm was dimmed by the fact that nothing whatsoever about the town looked familiar. It was small and well kept, so neat it almost looked like a storybook town.

Trees lined the streets, and many of the buildings had gingerbread trim. Quaint was definitely the word to describe it.

In the center of town was a small park. Workers were setting up a carnival there. Funny, she thought. It seems kind of chilly for a carnival.

Still, Alicia hoped she could talk Marta into going. It wasn't good, the way Marta never saw friends of her own or went out at night. All she ever did was come right home from that executive job of hers, and spend time with her sister.

Just as Alicia was thinking about Marta's executive job, she walked past the glass doors of the Grimly Public Library. There was Marta. She was pushing a cart piled high with books.

Staring with wide-eyed fascination, Alicia watched as Marta disappeared down aisle after aisle, then reappeared with a few less books on the cart. She did this until all the books were gone. Then she returned to the desk and loaded the cart with more books and started down the aisles again.

Alicia walked away from the library slowly,

full of jumbled emotions and confused thoughts. Why did Marta lie to me? she asked herself. It made her angry, the way Marta was always talking about sisters sticking together, and then lying.

Big executive job. Ha! She's shelving books at the library. Wait till I tell her that I'm on to her.

After walking a bit more, though, Alicia decided that maybe she wouldn't tell Marta she knew she'd lied about her job. Marta had done her best to take care of her, and she'd probably told her she had an important job to impress her. If I tell Marta that I saw her shelving books, she'll be embarrassed. That wouldn't be very nice. Besides, she thought, there was nothing so terrible about telling a little fib to impress your sister.

The clock outside the Grimly Savings Bank said two o'clock. There was still time to do some more shopping, buy groceries, and get home before Marta.

As she walked past a pet store, the sight of puppies in the window caught Alicia's attention. She couldn't resist going in for a closer look.

Inside, the puppies were in a large bin. They

tumbled over each other as they played with rubber toys.

"Cute, aren't they?" said an eager-faced clerk. "They're terriers. A terrific buy."

"They're adorable," Alicia agreed. "But not today."

"If they're too expensive, we have some very cute kittens we're practically giving away."

"Oh, it's not the price," Alicia told him. "I mean, it is and it isn't." It's Marta, she thought. Marta would have a fit if I brought one home.

The eagerness faded from the clerk's face. "Just looking?"

Alicia was about to answer yes, when the sight of a cage of canaries stopped her. Without thinking, she found herself saying, "No, I'm not just looking. I want one of *those*. That one." She pointed to a golden yellow bird with wings that were almost orange.

As she selected a cage and watched boxes of seed and other things for the bird pile up on the counter, Alicia silenced the whispered warning in her head that Marta wasn't going to like this.

Who couldn't like a canary? They were no

trouble at all, and their singing was lovely.

Besides, there was something familiar about canaries. I've had one before, Alicia thought. She was sure of it.

She whistled as she picked up the small covered cage and carried it outside. And then she stopped dead in her tracks.

The scar-faced man had reappeared. He was standing directly across from the store, smoking a cigarette.

As soon as he saw Alicia, he threw the cigarette on the ground. Then he ran toward her.

Chapter 15

Alicia ran. She had an unexplainable feeling that she knew the man with the scar on his face, and that the reason she knew him wasn't a good one.

She turned a corner, then another one, and ducked into the first store she could. It was a video store. Without pausing she went straight to the back and crouched down behind the counter. The bird started to sing.

"Hey, what's going on?" someone asked in a deep voice.

Alicia raised her eyes. She saw a boy about seventeen years old, tall, with shoulders that were broad for his slight frame. His long, light-brown hair fell over his collar. There was a small silver hoop in one ear.

"Since you're not speaking, I'll have to ask the question again. What's going on?" The boy smiled at her, revealing a row of dazzling white teeth.

"I'm hiding from a man who's been following me. He has the weirdest brown eyes and a big scar on his face."

The boy tilted his head to one side. "I can't believe it. I'm always seeing things like this happen in the movies. Now it's finally happening to *me*."

"It's *true*. I've seen him watching me. He was in the pizzeria, and then he followed me to a pet store."

The boy chuckled.

"What's so funny?" Alicia made an attempt to sound dignified. As soon as the boy had laughed, she'd had a sudden mental picture of herself running through the store, canary cage swinging on her arm. I must look ridiculous, she thought, wishing the floor would open and swallow her up.

"Never mind." The boy crouched down behind the counter beside her.

"Hello there. Nice of you to stop by and visit. My name's Mark Phillips."

"Alicia Taylor." The name came out in a whisper.

"Well, Alicia, why don't you come back into the office and tell me some more of this story.

You can hide just as well in there, and you'll be much more comfortable sitting in a chair. Oh, and you can bring your canary." Mark stood up and motioned for Alicia to follow him.

Alicia got up cautiously and peered over the counter. The store was empty. She followed Mark back to the tiny office.

"Wait just a minute. I'll go lock the door so you can relax," he said.

When he returned to the office, Alicia had seated herself in one of the folding chairs and placed the canary cage on the table. He's definitely good-looking, she thought, deciding that he was even taller than he seemed at first.

"So, tell me about the mysterious man with a scar on his face."

Alicia tucked a strand of hair behind her ear and took a deep breath. "Like I told you. I first saw him at Ken's pizzeria. Then I saw him walking behind me, but I lost him at Daisy Drugs. I started to think that maybe he wasn't even following me at all — until I left the pet store and he was standing right outside. He even started walking over to me."

Mark looked thoughtful. "Well — he could be a weirdo, all right. But it might have even been a coincidence that you saw him around all those times. Are you absolutely sure that he was running after you? Is there a chance you were being a bit jumpy?"

"You think I was being crazy, is that it?"

Mark shook his head. "No. I didn't mean that at all. It always pays to be careful, just in case. I'm just not convinced one hundred percent that the guy *definitely* was a threat."

Alicia thought for a moment, and then gave a little shrug. "Oh. Well, I guess that's possible."

Alicia noticed Mark studying her face.

"Do I have a smudge, or something caught between my teeth?"

"No — sorry if I was staring. You look familiar, that's all."

Alicia stared back at him. "Is that a line? Please tell me if it is, because you don't know how much it would mean to me to meet someone who knows me."

"Really?" Mark looked at her quizzically. "Why is that?"

Alicia shook her head. "Forget that I said that. It's complicated."

"Well, anyway, it's no line. I'm serious. At first I wasn't certain it was you. But now I am. I haven't seen you for a while, but I remember you, all right. I'll never forget how I saw you at the carnival one night when I was in junior high. I was in the eighth grade, and I was convinced that I was in love with you."

"Oh, come on," Alicia laughed.

"It's true," Mark said, holding up his right hand. "I saw you at the very same carnival they're setting up right now." He smiled. "It comes back every year. It's kind of funny, because it always comes around when it's just a bit early for a carnival, and so it's always too cold. But people always go, just the same."

As Mark spoke, he looked steadily into Alicia's eyes. "I looked for you at school, but I guess you go to private school or something."

"You really do remember me!"

"Absolutely! I remember seeing you another time. My parents turned this place into a video store when they bought it five years ago." Mark leaned back in his chair.

"I've been working here ever since. I pretty much run the place," he said, drawing himself up straighter.

"Very impressive," Alicia said, a smile playing about her lips. Marta wasn't the only one who liked to seem important.

"Anyway, it used to be an ice-cream parlor. I saw you one day sitting on a stool here —

and I almost got up the nerve to talk to you — but then you left. I bet you don't even remember."

Alicia shrugged. She didn't want to tell him exactly *how much* she didn't remember.

"Hey, I'll show you. Come on out — it's safe. The door's locked, remember?" He stood up.

"Okay." Alicia followed him from the office and out into the store.

"Look. The counter is still here. My parents kept it. They always talk about getting the ice cream going again. But they never get around to it. You know, it could be a combination video and ice-cream store. Great idea, huh?"

"Sure." Alicia walked up close, running her hand along the counter. So, years ago she had sat right here. He remembered her.

She tried to imagine herself sitting there, years ago. It might as well have happened to someone else, she thought.

Then suddenly, the memory came to her. So clear, so vivid, as if on a movie screen in her mind. There she was, wearing denim shorts and a red blouse, her feet clad in bright new sneakers. She even remembered that she had had a soda and a bowl of strawberry ice cream.

And she remembered him — off to one side with a friend.

"I remember you! You were standing with a friend who wore glasses."

"Skippy Murphy. Yeah. And I didn't think you noticed me."

"Oh — but I did. You've changed."

Alicia was enjoying talking to Mark so much she almost forgot about the time. But then her eyes rested on the clock above the cash register.

"Oh — it's getting late. I've got to get home."

She ran back into the office and grabbed the canary cage.

"Thanks for — well, it was good to meet you. Thanks for remembering me." She ran toward the door.

"Hey, wait a minute! I've got to unlock it, remember?" He walked over and turned the key. "Look, why don't you just wait a while, and I'll walk you home. It's only an hour until I get off work. I wouldn't want you to run into that weirdo."

"Oh, I'll be careful. But I've got to go right now. Thanks for everything." She hurried to the door, opened it, and rushed out.

"Hey, wait! Can't I have your phone number at least?" Mark came after her.

"Uh — the phone's out of order. I'll stop by and visit you again soon, though. 'Bye!"

"Well . . . see ya," Mark called after her.

Alicia walked as fast as she could and was relieved that she made it home before Marta, with nearly an hour to spare. And her ankle hardly hurt at all.

She moved some figurines from an end table to a shelf in the kitchen to make room for the canary. She got the bird thoroughly set up, and there was still over half an hour before Marta would get home.

There was a stack of puzzle books on the coffee table. Alicia sat down on the couch and opened one. Barely a minute passed before she tossed the book back on the table and sighed.

These things are *so boring*! she thought with exasperation. I've tried and tried to like them, but I just *don't*, no matter how much Marta says I do. And no matter how many times she tells me I'm a nice quiet girl who doesn't care about having boyfriends and likes to stay home all the time, it *just doesn't feel right*.

She began pacing aimlessly around the

room, opening cabinets and drawers. At first she only did it out of boredom and idle curiosity, but after a few moments the thought formed in her mind that she might discover something that would jog her memory — a letter, a postcard — *something*.

Alicia opened the drawers in the cabinets underneath the shelves where Marta kept the games. They were full of papers. Most of them looked like old tax forms and records, but she didn't dare take the time to go through everything now. She'd have to look more carefully later.

Then she remembered a briefcase she'd seen in the hall closet when she'd been looking for the telephone. She hurried to the closet and located the briefcase on the top shelf.

The briefcase wasn't securely locked. When Alicia grabbed the handle to pull it down, the case turned over. The contents spilled on the floor.

Alicia gasped. She was staring at a pile of watches, rings and other jewelry, at least a dozen checkbooks, and bundles of credit cards held together with rubber bands.

Chapter 16

"So now you know."

Startled, Alicia looked up to see Marta standing in the doorway. She took off her coat and came closer.

"Where did all this stuff come from?" Alicia asked.

Marta shrugged. "How should I know? Maybe you can tell me." Her eyes glittered.

Alicia looked at Marta's face as if searching for a clue. "I don't understand. Maybe I just don't remember."

Marta made a noise like a laugh, except that there was nothing happy about it — it sounded angry and nasty.

"What's going on?" Alicia asked. "This stuff must be *stolen*."

"Oh, my." Marta made the laugh noise again. "You don't remember." Her voice was heavy with sarcasm. She bent down and began scooping the jewelry and checkbooks back into the briefcase. "Of course this stuff is stolen, dear. You stole it. That's the deep, dark secret your sister's been keeping from you. Are you happy now?"

"I'm a thief?" Alicia gasped. It isn't possible, she thought. The shock of Marta's words had swept through her like a jolt of electricity.

Marta kept scooping items into the briefcase. "Phooey! I was hoping to spare you this. I wasn't sure if you'd remember. I suppose I wasn't really thinking clearly. I just wanted things to be different.

"I thought that maybe the amnesia was a kind of blessing," Marta continued. "I thought if I told you that you were a nice, quiet girl that maybe you'd start to be that way. Oh, I guess I knew it wouldn't work." She looked at Alicia with glaring, angry eyes. "But it might have worked, if you hadn't started snooping."

"Well, you might as well tell me the truth now, Marta."

"Fine," Marta snapped. "We'll just get all this fiddle-faddle out of the way." She finished putting the last of the things back in the briefcase and replaced it on the closet shelf. When she spoke, her words shot out angrily.

"Stealing was a regular routine for you. It started when you were a child. Then you were good for a while, and Mom and Dad thought you'd straightened out. But as soon as you got to be a teenager, *bang* . . . you were at it worse than ever. Off you went." Marta snapped her fingers in the air.

"And that's not all," she continued. "You were always getting into trouble at school, throwing temper tantrums, making public scenes, running around with a wild crowd . . ."

Marta glared into Alicia's eyes. "You even spent some time in a mental hospital."

"No . . ." Alicia took a step backward.

"Yes! And I know the gang of low-life troublemakers you call your friends would love to see you again. You double-crossed one of them and didn't give them their part of the cash you got with a stolen credit card. They're looking for you. Since you don't remember, I'll tell you that your friends hang around with some serious criminals — tough people."

Immediately, the image of the scar-faced man flashed into Alicia's mind. He certainly *looked* tough enough to be a criminal.

"I told your friends they'd better not come around here," Marta went on. She clenched and unclenched her fists at her sides as she spoke. "I thought maybe if you'd just stayed at home, they'd forget about you, and maybe you'd change. . . ." Marta crossed her arms. "I'm tired of covering for you and taking care of you. I'm tired of people saying I'm the one with the crazy sister."

Alicia was horrified. Her mind was filled with disbelief, mingled with dread that what Marta was saying was true. She struggled to find something to say to Marta.

But Marta's attention had turned from Alicia to something else.

"What's this?" she demanded, eyes blazing. Her finger was pointing to the canary. "What's this?" she said again, louder this time.

In spite of the fury blazing in Marta's eyes, Alicia had to stifle the urge to laugh. "A canary?" she ventured. It seemed obvious enough.

"I know it's a canary!" Marta said, stamping her foot. "What I mean is, what's it doing here?"

"I bought it. I passed this pet store and I saw how cute the dogs and cats were. But I knew I shouldn't get one of those without talking to you first — but then I saw this bird and

— and I didn't think anyone could mind a little bird. Look — it's so small. It will be nice to have a pet."

"You took money to buy this? You're stealing again?"

"Well I — " Alicia stammered. Then she lifted her chin. "I'll pay it back. What are you so angry about, anyway? What happened to 'sisters sticking together'?"

Marta glanced at the bird with a look of disgust. "This cage can't stay here," she said, grabbing it and depositing it roughly in an armchair.

Alicia watched as she strode briskly into the kitchen and came back with both hands full of figurines. She proceeded to arrange them on the table exactly as they had been before.

While she arranged the figurines, Marta looked as if she was in a trance. When she was finished she stood back and studied them, then repositioned some figures. "There!" she said finally, smiling for the first time since coming in the door.

But when she turned to Alicia, the smile was gone. "What do you need a pet for? Isn't everything nice enough here? Don't I get you everything you need?"

"Sometimes it gets lonely in here. I just wanted some company."

Marta faced her with a resentful sneer. "No matter how hard I try, nothing is ever good enough for you. You can't stay out of trouble! You made so much trouble for Mom and Dad — and now when I try to keep you from getting into more trouble, you won't cooperate." Alicia watched Marta's fists opening and closing at her sides. Marta took several deep breaths, and then turned to walk away.

Suddenly, she wheeled around and turned back to Alicia. "Did you talk to anyone while you were in town?" Her eyes blazed even more angrily than before.

In an instant, Alicia decided it was best not to tell the truth.

"No."

"Are you sure?"

"Yes. I'm sure."

Alicia could see Marta relax. "Good. You shouldn't. I'm only telling you that for your own good."

"But *why*?"

"Shut up! Just do what you're supposed to. Stay home, don't talk to anyone, don't make any trouble, and everything will be okay."

"Okay," Alicia said, although she didn't mean it. She just wanted Marta to calm down. The way she was acting was scary.

Marta stared at her with a brittle stare. "I suppose I didn't realize your ankle was so much better." She tilted her head to one side.

"Yes, it's much better. I'm feeling better overall, Marta. Now I can help you out around the house, so you won't have to do everything yourself. Look — let me finish making dinner for you. Just sit and relax."

"I'll finish dinner. I know the way I like things done."

"Marta, please. I'd like to help out."

Alicia was surprised and relieved when Marta agreed. She sat at the table and watched everything she did like a hawk, and made her so nervous she was sure she'd drop something. Somehow, she didn't.

Finally the meal was ready. Hamburger patties, green beans, boiled potatoes. Alicia would have preferred some fish and fresh salad, but she had to work with what she had. After her adventures this afternoon she'd completely forgotten about her plans to get groceries.

She put the food on the table and smiled at Marta. "I hope you like it."

Marta smiled back, and then, without warning, she picked up her plate and threw it against the wall. Bits of hamburger and grease stuck there. Jagged pieces of plate bounced to the floor, along with pieces of potato and green beans.

"There! See what you made me do!" she screamed. Then she turned strangely quiet, as if all the force had blown out of her. "Maybe you'll decide the dinners I make are good enough after all," she said quietly. Then she went upstairs. Alicia heard her slamming the door to her room.

Hours later, Alicia tossed and turned in bed. She could not get the scene at dinner out of her mind. Marta had looked so strange.

Afterward, Alicia had cleaned up the mess. Then she found she was unable to eat her own dinner. She had put it in the refrigerator.

Now her stomach growled.

She got out of bed and put on a robe, moving quietly so as not to disturb Marta.

As soon as Alicia opened the door to her room, she felt the draft. The temperature got colder and colder as she crept down the stairs. By the time she got to the living room, she was freezing.

Every window in the room was wide open.

Cold air was rushing in on all sides.

Shivering, teeth chattering, Alicia ran from window to window, closing them.

It was only then that she saw the light from the window falling on the canary cage. The cover had slipped down and she could see that inside, the canary was lying on the floor of the cage. The cold had killed it.

Chapter 17

Alicia's appetite vanished when she saw the dead canary. For a long time, she was unable to take her eyes off the bird. A dull, jellied lump of terror formed in her stomach. The bird's death was no accident. She was sure of that. It was cold outside — there was no logical reason to open the windows. Now it was freezing in the room.

The poor little bird, she thought. Marta made it the victim of her anger against *me*. How could she be so cruel? *It isn't only cruel — it's weird,* she said to herself.

Alicia went back to bed and fell into a fitful sleep. In her dreams she ran down the tunnel again, pursued by the fierce, shadowy figure. The dream was no less terrifying because of its familiarity.

When the nightmare faded she tossed and

turned, somewhere between sleep and waking. Several times she thought she felt hands touch her hair, but the feeling hovered on the edge of her sleep.

Then the sound of Marta's voice jerked her awake.

"There! With your hair cut off, it won't be so easy for someone to recognize you if you go sneaking out again."

She held up a handful of Alicia's hair, her lips drawn back from her teeth in an eerie grin. "Now everything's hunky-dory."

Frantically, Alicia touched her hands to her scalp. She felt short, spiky tufts of hair.

She jumped from the bed and ran to the mirror. Her reflection horrified her. Her hair stuck out all over her head in uneven clumps.

She blinked, and the reflection changed. Her hair hung to her shoulders just as it had before.

She shook her head quickly and looked again. Her hair was still the same length.

Alicia took a long, deep breath and exhaled. After a few moments she realized what had happened. Her mind had played a trick on her.

She had only dreamed that Marta came in and chopped off her hair. The dream had been so scary, so vivid, so real, that at first she hadn't known where the dream *stopped*, and what she saw when she was awake *started*. For an instant, her mind was convinced that the dream was *real*.

She sat down on the edge of her bed and cradled her head in her hands. She had pushed her mistrust of Marta to the back of her mind, but could ignore it no longer. Plus, she had grown fearful of her. The dream was proof of that.

Marta had admitted that she'd told her lies, but Alicia wasn't convinced that she had finally told her the truth. She just couldn't believe she was a thief. She couldn't imagine why Marta would lie about such a thing, though.

She raked a hand through her hair. There had to be a way to find some answers. But where could she turn? Then she had an idea.

"Can I speak with Dr. Kellogg, please?"

The nurse behind the hospital desk looked harried and distracted. So did the other three nurses behind the desk. Since she ignored Alicia the first time, it was necessary to repeat the question.

"Excuse me," Alicia raised her voice, "I need to see Dr. Kellogg."

This time the nurse looked up. Her face wore a pinched expression of annoyance.

"Do you have an appointment?"

Alicia shook her head. "No — but I really need to see her. It's terribly important."

The nurse went back to her paperwork. She spoke without even looking at Alicia. "The doctor is too busy. You'll have to call for an appointment."

"Please, can't you just check? I came all the way over here, and it's very important."

The woman looked up sharply. "I told you the doctor is too busy. We can't have everybody just waltzing in off the street to see her. You'll have to call and make an appointment."

Alicia tapped her foot impatiently. She hoped that Dr. Kellogg could tell her something about her hospital stay that would help her sort things out. She didn't have much hope, but she didn't know what else to try. She just *had to* talk to her.

"Look, *please*, can't you just check with Dr. Kellogg?"

The nurse slapped the counter with her palm. "What's the matter with you? Don't you understand that you have to call for an appointment?"

"It doesn't make any sense to call to make an appointment if I'm already here," Alicia snapped. "Why can't I just make the appointment now?"

"Because you have to *call*. That's the way it's done," the nurse snapped.

Alicia gave an exasperated sigh. Then she heard a voice behind her. "Alicia! I didn't think we'd ever see you again!"

Alicia turned around and came face-to-face with Dr. Kellogg.

"Oh, Dr. Kellogg. I'm so glad to see you! I need to ask you some questions — but they told me you were too busy."

Dr. Kellogg nodded wearily. "That's always true. But perhaps we can talk a little, if you don't mind walking while we do it. I'm on my way to look in on a patient."

"I don't care if we *run*, as long as I can talk to you."

Dr. Kellogg smiled. Alicia's heart sank when she saw that it was the beaming, game-show hostess kind of smile she'd seen before. She looked the doctor in the eye.

"Please, Dr. Kellogg, whatever you do, don't just nod and smile and tell me not to worry the way you did when I was in the hospital. I'm desperate."

The smile vanished from Dr. Kellogg's face. "All right," she said after a moment. "It sounds like you have some very important questions." She started walking down the corridor, and Alicia followed at her side.

"You know, Alicia, I called your house several times and never got an answer. We were trying to monitor your progress. Then finally I got hold of your sister, and she told me you were away visiting relatives."

So that's who called when I overheard Marta on the phone, Alicia said to herself. "Well, Dr. Kellogg, I *wasn't* visiting relatives. That's kind of what I wanted to talk to you about. It's all so confusing, I hardly know where to begin."

"It certainly sounds confusing," Dr. Kellogg agreed. "I don't understand why Marta would tell me you went away, when you didn't. Before you left the hospital, I spoke with her and told her you should come in each week for follow-up visits."

"It's strange, all right," Alicia said. "I know I'm grasping at straws, but can you recall anything I said while I was in the hospital that stood out? I'm looking for something that might trigger a memory."

Dr. Kellogg shook her head. "I'm sorry. I wish I could help."

Alicia looked away and sighed. "I suppose that's what I expected." She looked at Dr. Kellogg. "It's such a wild, incredible thing. I woke up one day and found out that I'd been in a coma for four months . . . and I'd forgotten who I was."

Suddenly Dr. Kellogg stopped walking and turned to Alicia. Her face wore a stunned expression. "Alicia, why in the world would you think that you were in a coma for four months? Is that what your sister told you?"

Alicia nodded, her heart beating faster.

"Alicia, you were only in the hospital for a few days."

Chapter 18

Why would Marta tell me I'd been in a coma for four months when I'd only been in the hospital for a few days? Alicia asked herself again and again as she left the hospital.

By the time she got on the bus and was headed for Grimly, she had put together some possible answers that she didn't like very much.

If I'd been in a coma for four months, then the idea that I shouldn't return to school seems more believable than if I'd only been out for a short while. Marta made up the lie to make it easier to keep me at home, away from everyone.

If I had been in a coma for four months, wouldn't my leg have been healed? After all, I didn't break it, and it was better after I'd been home for a week. And why would it have taken Marta months to find me, when I was in a hospital *in the same county where we live*? How could I have been so gullible? she asked herself.

Now that I've found out about all the lies Marta told me — what next? And what about the stolen credit cards and jewelry?

Alicia looked out at the trees floating past as the bus moved down the highway. If only I could remember, she wailed inwardly.

The bus drew closer to the town of Grimly, and Alicia knew what she would do. She would visit Mark and talk to him.

When Mark saw Alicia enter the video store, a wide smile spread across his face. "Hi! The way you ran off that time, I was afraid I was never going to see you again."

"Well, here I am. Can we talk?"

Mark came out from behind the counter. "You bet we can! My younger brother is here. He can watch the store for a while." Mark leaned across the counter. "Hey, Joe — you're on your own. I'll be back in a bit." He grabbed Alicia's arm. "Come on, let's get going."

"Hey — wait a minute. You can't leave me here alone," called a voice from the back of the store.

"Oh, you'll do fine," Mark called back. "Let's hurry," he whispered to Alicia.

Once outside the store, Mark kept walking fast until they were at the end of the block. "What's the idea?" Alicia asked.

Mark smiled. "I wanted to get away before Joe could give me a hard time about leaving the store. He plays the same trick on me sometimes."

They turned the corner, and Mark grabbed Alicia's hand and gave it a squeeze. "I'm so glad to see you. I've been thinking about you ever since I saw you the other day. I told you I thought I was in love with you years ago. I think I've had a crush on you since then." Mark leaned closer to her . . . much closer. He was leaning down to kiss her.

"Hey, hey, not so fast," Alicia said, putting a restraining hand on his chest. The image of the dark-haired boy from her dreams flashed before her eyes. She glanced down at her hand in Mark's and withdrew it from his grasp.

Mark stepped back. "Okay, okay. Sorry." There was an impish smile on his face.

"Mark, I've got to talk to you."

"It sounds serious," Mark said, looking into her eyes.

"It is." Alicia looked back at him. "Let's take a walk over to the park."

Mark nodded and followed her to the little park in the center of town. They took a seat on a bench.

Alicia's thoughts whirled. She wanted to tell him about the amnesia . . . to blurt everything out. Yet she was afraid to. What if Mark thought she was nuts? Alicia clenched her fists in her lap.

"There are some really weird things going on in my life," she said. "And I've got to talk to someone."

Mark nodded.

Alicia bit her lip. "This is going to sound pretty strange, but I was in a car accident and I hit my head. Ever since then, I've had amnesia."

She looked at Mark quickly. His eyes were wide with surprise, but he was still sitting there. He hadn't jumped up and run away, or yelled that she was out of her mind.

"I just can't imagine what that's like. Frightening, I'm sure. You don't remember anything?"

Alicia gave a little shrug. "I've remembered

a few things. Just bits and pieces. Anyway, I've been staying with my sister. She told me my parents were killed in the same car accident that gave me the amnesia."

"I'm so sorry about your parents." Mark laid a hand gently on her arm.

Alicia shook her head. "Thanks. But it's pretty strange. I don't remember them yet."

Now that she'd started her story, Alicia resolved to finish it. "The problem is my sister. I know she's lying to me about a lot of things, but I'm not sure why. She doesn't want me to talk on the phone or leave the house, either. She'd have a fit if she knew I was here right now." Alicia's words were tumbling out faster and faster.

"My sister Marta lies about everything. She even lied about her job. She kept talking about being a big executive — but I saw her shelving books in the library . . ."

"Hold it!" Mark interrupted suddenly. "Your sister's name is Marta, and she works in the library?"

"That's right," Alicia nodded. "Why? Do you know my sister?"

Mark shook his head and ran a hand through his hair.

"No — but I know *about* her."

He looked at Alicia with an appraising stare. "It seems impossible that she's your sister. It must have been tough growing up with her. Everybody knows that she's completely crazy."

Chapter 19

Mark stopped speaking suddenly. "I'm sorry," he murmured after a moment. "I shouldn't have said that about your sister."

Alicia let out a long sigh. "I suppose I should be angry . . . but somehow, I'm not. I'm starting to think she's crazy, too."

Mark looked concerned as he spoke. "Maybe you shouldn't go home, Alicia. Listen, I'm sorry to say this about your sister, but she's done some pretty strange things. Every so often she has some kind of wild temper tantrum in public." He lowered his voice to a hush. "People have suspected her of stealing for years. I think some people even *knew* she stole things, but kept quiet because they felt sorry for her."

"The briefcase!" Alicia blurted out, looking at him with wide eyes. "I found a briefcase full of credit cards and checkbooks and jewels. Marta said I stole the things."

"You're kidding!" Mark was shaking his head. "I don't believe it, Alicia. I'd sooner believe that she's the one who stole them. Listen, people have openly accused her of stealing more than once. They could never prove it — but then . . ." Mark's voice trailed off.

"Then what?"

"Well . . ." Mark looked at the ground. "It's complicated."

"Complicated?"

Mark was silent for a moment. He stuffed both hands into his pockets.

"Everybody knows Marta's got — problems. People feel sorry for her. The only reason she's even got that job in the library is because the librarian has known her since she was a little girl and wanted to help her."

Mark paced back and forth a few times. "If people knew she'd stolen so many things, they might think differently." He stood close to Alicia. "Really — I think she could be dangerous. I'm asking you again not to go home."

"Oh, come on, Mark." Alicia got to her feet. "She may be weird, but I don't think she'd hurt me. Besides, if I don't go home, where would I go? I don't have any money . . . and I don't have any memory. Look, I'll come back and visit you soon." She looked up at the clock on the Grimly Savings Bank. "I've got to go."

Mark called after her twice as she walked away. She didn't turn around. She was thinking of what she was going to say to Marta.

The house was quiet. Alicia was glad she'd have time to organize her thoughts and decide what she wanted to say before Marta got home. It should be at least an hour before she arrived.

Alicia walked through the kitchen and into the living room. She passed the table full of figurines where she had placed the canary cage just a while ago. Something on the table caught her eye.

It was a new figurine . . . *a canary*. Its newness stood out among the other figurines that now had a thin film of dust. So did the table. Alicia took a step away from the table and swallowed hard. She turned and headed up the stairs.

At the top of the stairs she paused before turning into her own room. Marta's door was open.

"Marta?" Alicia called softly — then again, louder. "Marta?"

When there was no answer, she pushed the door open and stepped inside. She gave a little gasp of surprise. Marta's tidiness had slipped a bit in the rest of the house, but here it had fallen off the edge. Dust balls decorated the corners and peeked from under the bed. There must have been at least a hundred figurines jumbled in confusion all over the dresser and night table. Dust coated them like fur.

Marta'a shoes and clothes were everywhere — on the floor, on the bed, and even on the windowsill. No wonder she's been looking a little disheveled lately, Alicia thought.

A little shiver ran down her spine as she looked at the scene. The state of the room was concrete evidence that Marta had been losing it for a while, and losing it big time.

Alicia pulled open the drawer in the bedside table. She almost laughed at her good fortune. Inside the drawer was Marta's diary.

Her elation vanished in an instant. The diary was probably locked. If she tampered with it, Marta was sure to know.

She picked the diary up and examined it. Her heart skipped a beat. The lock was *already broken*. Marta probably thought she didn't have to worry about keeping the diary locked because she always locked her door.

But not today. Today she forgot, Alicia said gleefully to herself. Her heart beating faster, she leaned against the wall and opened the diary. With trembling hands she opened the diary and began to read.

She was surprised that the diary started on the day Marta had brought Alicia home from the hospital.

Now my little sister is home. I can take care of her, and we'll be together always.

She turned a page.

Alicia doesn't remember a thing. I will make her memories for her.

Alicia turned page after page about how the two of them played games together and other trivial details. It was pretty boring. But then the entries started getting angry.

She doesn't appreciate anything I do. She'd better start to change . . . selfish . . . ungrateful. She's not the sister I wanted.

The next page made Alicia's scalp prickle. The page was scrawled all over with words that were carved deep into the page in red ink.

I hate my sister. I hate my sister. I hate my sister.

Taking a deep breath, Alicia turned the page

and read on. The more she read, the more terrified she became.

The entire diary was about her.

And then she came to a page that chilled her to the bone.

I kept hoping Alicia would change and become the sister I wanted. I gave her every chance, but now I know she won't. I'm going to have to kill her.

Alicia gave a little cry and started to run from the room. Only then did she see that Marta was standing in the doorway, watching her. She was holding a carving knife.

Chapter 20

"I was just going to fix you a sandwich," Marta said, her eyes twinkling and an eerie smile playing about her lips. She turned the blade of the carving knife this way and that as Alicia stared, paralyzed with fear.

"When I called and called, I came looking for you." Marta's expression was mocking. "Yikes! I guess you were so engrossed in your reading you didn't hear me." Her voice turned into an angry snarl. "Did you find my diary interesting reading? You shouldn't read other people's diaries. Shame, shame on you." She took a step toward Alicia, waving the knife in front of her.

Alicia dropped the diary and screamed. She lifted her hands in front of her face.

Marta's eyes blazed. "Everything always turned out all right for you. Off you went with your friends. You forgot all about me. Well, it's not going to turn out like that this time," she hissed.

"What are you going to do?" Alicia whispered, terrified.

"You read my diary, didn't you?" Marta replied, in a whisper.

Without thinking about what she was doing, Alicia acted blindly, driven by a mixture of terror and rage. She shoved her shoulder against Marta's and pushed her aside.

Surprised, Marta was caught off guard and stumbled. It gave Alicia a moment to start racing down the stairs.

In an instant, she heard Marta running behind her. The blade of the carving knife hissed as it lashed the air.

Alicia leaped down the stairs two and three at a time, praying that she could open the door before Marta caught her.

Soon, however, she knew it was not to be.

The moment when she lost her balance went by in a blinding flash and in slow motion at the same time. Too late she realized she was going to fall, and understood the reason. She saw her toe reach for the stair below and watched it brush the figurine of a leaping cat that had been left there. In the same twisted moment, she knew that Marta must have put it there so she would fall.

The moment vanished, and Alicia continued falling until she landed in a heap at the bottom of the stairs. She dreaded the slashing of the knife that she expected to come. Instead, Marta grabbed her roughly by the collar and began pulling her along the floor, the carpet burning her outstretched palms.

She's dragging me toward the basement, Alicia realized. She tried to grab one of Marta's legs and pull her off balance, but it was impossible. Marta was much bigger than Alicia and solidly built. Plus, she was fueled with the energy of madness.

Soon, Marta was opening the basement door. She gave a heave that sent Alicia half stumbling, half falling down the basement steps.

She landed on the cold concrete floor and heard Marta slam the door shut. "You stay down there until I figure out how I'm going to kill you," she heard Marta shrieking on the other side of the door. "It's what you deserve for being such a selfish, ungrateful sister. After everything I did for you, you had to have your other friends and your dances and parties. You won't be having any more. Just think about that!"

Alicia curled up into a ball on the floor and listened to Marta's insane raving. It went on for what seemed like hours. Finally, Alicia fell asleep.

When she awoke, it was quiet. Slowly and painfully, she uncurled herself and tried to sit up. Every part of her body felt achy and sore.

I'm bruised and banged up all right, but nothing's broken, she decided when she'd finally managed to get herself into a sitting position.

The light was on now, so Marta must have opened the door and switched it on while she was sleeping. Somehow, she knew that the switch was at the top of the steps by the door.

Alicia looked up and saw that Marta had left something for her near the top of the stairs. It was a tray with a covered dish on it.

Only then did Alicia realize that she was famished and terribly thirsty. Her stomach growled emptily as she got up. Her hunger overshadowed her pain, and she hardly noticed her bruises as she crawled up the stairs toward the tray.

She eased herself onto the step beside the dish. First, she picked up the glass filled with water and drank several huge gulps. Instantly, the water made her feel more awake and alive.

Her stomach rumbled again. She set down the glass and lifted the cover off the dish.

Alicia whirled and turned her head away from the sight of what was on the dish. She had a sickening feeling that she knew how Marta was planning to kill her. She was going to starve her to death.

Under the covered dish was a small bird, lying on a bed of lettuce. The bird must have been kept in the freezer, because it was frozen solid.

It was Alicia's dead canary.

Chapter 21

"How did you like breakfast?" Alicia heard Marta chuckling outside the locked basement door. Nearly an hour had passed since she'd discovered the dead canary. She'd placed it, dish and all, in a bin she'd found in the corner of the basement.

"Come on, Alicia," the gloating voice called again. "Talk to your sister. I can't decide what to fix you for lunch. Maybe you can give me some ideas. You must be getting hungry." The sound of Marta's laughter drifted down the stairs.

"Answer me, Alicia." Marta's voice had gotten meaner. "Tell me what you want for lunch. Unless you want me to use my imagination."

Sitting in a corner of the basement, Alicia rested her head in her hands. She wished Marta would just go away and leave her alone.

"Alicia!" Marta screeched. When there was no reply, she kicked the door hard. Then Alicia heard the sound of her footsteps clumping angrily away. Funny how Marta's footsteps are so loud and clumsy so often, yet when she wants to she can glide across the floor without making a sound, she thought.

Well, she left me alone, so I got my wish, I suppose, Alicia thought to herself. Giving in to despair wouldn't do anything for her. She had to keep calm, keep thinking clearly, and figure a way out of this.

A grim smile spread across her face. Why am I kidding myself? There's no way out of here. The basement windows are boarded shut. The only way to get free is to get past the maniac who wants to kill me. It's impossible.

Don't believe it, whispered a small, faint voice inside her head. Alicia sighed. Okay, she wouldn't give up, or believe that it was impossible to get out of here. But first she had to find a way to calm down, to quiet the terror that screamed inside and threatened to destroy her sanity.

Resolutely, Alicia rose to her feet and began walking around the basement. There wasn't much there but junk. No basement tool shop that might have contained something to use to defend herself against Marta.

No gardening tools were stored down here, either. What I wouldn't give for a hoe or a rake, Alicia thought.

As she walked, it occurred to her that Marta might even have been planning this for days. It would have given her time to clean out anything that could have been used as a weapon. After her third circuit of the basement, Alicia was convinced that Marta had done just that. Nothing had been left to chance.

Wearily, she sat down again. Lying on the floor next to her was a roll of paper, the kind used to line drawers and shelves. She picked it up and tore off a piece. Digging into her pocket, she fished out a pen and began to scribble on it, doodling absently. If only I could draw an open window and crawl through it, she thought, remembering a cartoon she'd seen somewhere.

Soon the doodles became more intricate designs. Gradually, she felt excitement building. Then it was as if a switch had been thrown and light flooded her mind.

Hurriedly, she made a few more marks on the paper. Then she jumped to her feet.

There was a pile of old newspapers in one

corner of the basement. She grabbed several of them and placed them at her feet. Then she tore off another sheet of shelf paper and put it on top. Now, she said to herself as she sat down, I'll begin to really *draw*.

First she sketched the trash bin and pile of newspapers in one corner. Then she sketched the basement steps. And then she tried something different. A self-portrait from memory.

Time flew by as Alicia drew. She forgot her bruises and her hunger in her excitement. Even when hours later Marta stood screaming outside the basement door, she didn't hear her. She was totally consumed by what she was doing. She didn't know how long she kept making drawings, but when she finally stopped, there was a pile of them strewn around her on the basement floor.

Alicia flexed her right hand. It ached from holding the pen, which was beginning to run out of ink. Her legs were getting stiff. Slowly, she got to her feet and flexed her ankles several times to get the blood flowing through them again.

Suddenly, something in one of the corners caught her eye. It was some kind of sack, stuffed behind some broken wooden chairs.

The corner was so dark that she could hardly make out the shape of it.

It's not a sack, it's a leather bag of some sort, she realized. Alicia stared at it, her brain beginning to tingle.

She walked over to the corner and pulled the dusty black leather bag from behind the chairs. It's a *purse*, she said to herself, feeling a prickle of excitement along her spine.

She unzipped the purse and stuck her hand inside. She pulled out a wallet. Her heart hammering and her fingers trembling, she began examining the contents.

Her chest fairly exploded as she pulled out an ID card with her picture on it. *Alicia Fisher*, it read, *Shelbyville High School of Art and Design*.

Fisher, she repeated to herself. Alicia *Fisher*, not Alicia *Taylor*. Her whole body was shaking as she took out the other cards in the wallet. There was a driver's license, a library card, and another card that showed she was a member of the Jump! Athletic Club.

There were pictures in the wallet, too. A few of girls, and two of the dark-haired boy she'd seen in her dreams. Alicia clutched his picture tightly in her hand.

I remember, I remember, I remember, she whispered over and over. A vision of the dark-haired boy formed in her mind. You're my boyfriend, Alicia said to herself. Your name is Lou. We've been going together for two years, we both like to paint. You have a motorcycle, and you hate broccoli. Oh, where are you, Lou? I miss you so much!

Abruptly, the image of Lou vanished, and another vision flashed into her mind.

She saw herself standing outside with Marta. They were children. Both of them were laughing. Another little girl ran up to them, and in her mind's eye she could see Marta's expression cloud with anger. Marta began screaming at the little girl, who ran away, crying. Then Marta had chased after Alicia. There was a rock in her hand. . . .

The scene faded, and Alicia felt a shudder run through her body. I remember that day, Marta, she said to herself. The other little girl's name was Molly, and she wanted to play with us. But you didn't like other kids to play with us. It made you angry. And when I wanted the other kids to play it made you *very* angry.

They thought you'd outgrow it, but you didn't. When you got older you kept getting angrier and angrier, and more and more jealous of anyone I wanted for a friend. You started taking it out on me, and you didn't just scream . . . you hit. Finally we had to be kept apart.

Then a flash of understanding blazed through her. It filled her with dread. It's true what Mark said about you, Marta. You're crazy . . . she whispered to herself. Alicia clenched her hands in her lap as the thought finished . . . *and you're not my sister.*

Chapter 22

Marta and I were childhood friends.

The memory had been so far out of reach, yet now was easily within Alicia's grasp.

We pretended we were sisters. It was a game we played all the time.

A veil of darkness still covered the past, but it was fading now, piece by piece. She recalled clearly how she and Marta had lived next door to each other, in another town, the name of which she couldn't place just yet.

Marta and I were inseparable when we were children. Then Marta's parents moved about fifty miles away, to Grimly. Our parents chauffeured us back and forth every week or so until Marta's problems got worse . . . and worse. The visits became fewer and fewer.

When we were teenagers, we visited more frequently for a while. It started when Marta was in the mental hospital. Then she got out in a few months, and for a while it seemed she was better. It didn't last. Soon Marta was violent all over again.

On the cold cement floor, Alicia hugged her knees to her chest. A wave of fatigue swept over her, as if remembering had drained her of energy. She fell asleep on the cold concrete floor, her drawings strewn about her.

When Alicia awoke, an ashy light filtered through the gaps in the boards over the windows. She turned her head and saw two glittering eyes staring back at her. A scream tore from her throat as she realized that the eyes belonged to a rat that was watching her, its tail coiled neatly around its body.

At the sound of her scream, the rat fled. Alicia felt a thick, soupy terror at the thought of rats crawling over her body . . . even biting her as she slept.

She was sure she would never sleep again, but then weariness and weakness overtook her once more, and her eyes closed again. The walls of the basement faded away and she was in the arms of the dark-haired boy. He held her close against his chest, and in her dream she could feel the hardness of his muscles under the softness of his leather jacket. . . .

When Alicia woke again, the overhead light-bulb was glaring. Marta must have opened the door and turned it on again.

Hesitantly, Alicia looked up the basement steps to see if she had left another offering. She hadn't.

It was dark outside, that much she could see through the boarded windows. What time is it? she wondered. She was aware of a gnawing pain in her stomach and a parched feeling in her mouth. If Marta's not even going to give me anything to drink, death will come quickly, she thought. Already she felt a kind of delirium.

Painfully, she sat up and blinked as her eyes adjusted to the dim light. Where is the rat? she wondered.

Then she heard something that drove all thoughts of the rat from her mind. *Voices.*

"Sorry to wake you at this time of night — but you understand why we've got to find the girl as soon as possible," a gravelly voice boomed. Alicia's heart leaped.

"Oh, I'm happy to help." Marta's voice dripped with sincerity. She's laying it on too thick, Alicia thought. She wanted to scream, but could hardly breathe.

"I'm sure you are," the rasping tones replied in exaggerated politeness.

He knows something's up with her, Alicia whispered to herself with excitement. There was a roaring sound in her head.

"I really must ask you to let me get some sleep now, Detective. I have an important job to do tomorrow."

"Oh, yes, I understand completely." The masculine voice oozed with charm. "I'll get right out of your way . . . after I search the basement."

"Oh, come now, Detective! You don't really think that's necessary?" Marta's voice took on the panicky, high-pitched squeak it did when she was nervous. "I can't — I can't find the key."

When the detective spoke this time, he let Marta know the game was over. "Don't be afraid, Marta. You're not going to be put in prison — we only want to help you."

At the sound of the word "help," Alicia found her voice.

"Help!" she screamed, with all the strength she could muster. "Help! Get me out of here!"

In answer, there was a series of heavy thumps on the basement door. The detective was breaking it down. As the door flew open, Alicia was already bounding up the stairs.

"Get me away from *her*," she gasped as she bounded through the basement door into the kitchen. When she saw the man standing beside Marta, shock sparked through her. "Detective . . ." she whispered in amazement.

She was staring at the scar-faced man.

"Private investigator," he smiled. "Name's Jake Coyle. Your father hired me." The man's smile performed a miraculous transformation on his face, changing it in an instant from frightening to friendly. Beside him, Marta looked as if she'd turned off, somehow. Her expression was blank, as if she'd gone off somewhere and left her body behind.

"How did you find me?" Alicia breathed, her heart overflowing with relief and gratitude.

"A friend of yours by the name of Mark. The fellow that works in the video store in town." Jake Coyle's smile disappeared. "I wish he'd told the truth sooner. When I first showed him your picture, he said he'd never seen you. I told him where to get in touch with me if you turned up. I was surprised when he decided to change his story. It seems at first he thought he was protecting you."

"Thank goodness," Alicia said softly.

"I saw you in town, too. I wish you weren't so good at getting away."

"I was running from the wrong person." Alicia was beginning to feel woozy from her burst of exertion. "I should have been running from Marta."

Suddenly, Alicia's mind snapped into alertness. Her gaze darted around the kitchen. She didn't see Marta.

"Where's Marta?" Alicia said in a frightened whisper. "You have to watch out for her. She's crazy!"

Jake gave her a reassuring smile. "Don't you worry. I can handle Marta."

Alicia's jaw dropped as over Jake's shoulder, the specter of Marta appeared out of nowhere. She came creeping up behind him in the eerie, silent way she had.

Jake continued to smile at Alicia with quiet confidence. The words, "Look out!" were barely out of her mouth when the iron skillet in Marta's hand connected with his skull. There was a sickening thud. Alicia watched in horror as he collapsed like an inflatable doll that someone had let all the air out of.

Chapter 23

Alicia pressed the heel of her hand to her mouth as she saw the insane rage in Marta's eyes. It was as if there was no soul behind them. An animallike growl erupted from her throat as she raised the skillet over her head once more. The thought went through Alicia's mind that she must be very strong to do that with one hand.

Marta brought the skillet swinging down in an arc. She bent her knees, aiming for the prone body of the detective.

Already running for the door, Alicia screamed, "Don't!"

Marta's arm jerked to a stop. She looked up at Alicia with wild, startled eyes. Suddenly, she lost interest in bashing the detective. Instead, she sent the skillet crashing into a corner and chased after Alicia.

As she ran, Alicia overturned a chair in Marta's path. *"Ooomf!"* Marta grunted as she tripped over it. There was a hollow, metallic clang as Marta shoved the chair out of the way and it landed against the cabinet under the sink.

Alicia could hear her own breathing coming in heavy gasps as she reached for the knob on the kitchen door. Her hands were so damp with perspiration that they slipped as she tried to turn it. She heard Marta's footsteps running behind her.

"I'll tear you apart!" Marta screamed. Something struck a pane of glass in the kitchen doorway, shattering it. Marta had thrown a cup.

"Uuuuuhhhh," gasped Alicia as something struck her in the middle of her back. She's going to try to hit me in the head. The thought raced through her mind.

A dish shattered on the wall beside the kitchen door. Alicia managed to get a grip on the knob, turned, and yanked. In a second she ran through the doorway and into the garage.

She gave silent thanks when she saw the

garage door was open. Panting, she ran through it and out into the street and the inky darkness of the night.

In the hushed darkness, Alicia heard the sound of Marta's running footsteps. She didn't dare imagine how close she must be.

Screaming for help was impossible. It took every last bit of breath she had just to keep going.

She kept running, turning the corner at the end of the block. She went past the darkened pizzeria. Gates were pulled down over the entrance.

What time can it be? Alicia wondered. Eleven at night? Or three in the morning? If I make it into town without Marta catching me, what then? If everything's shut up tight, how will I find help?

The headlights of an approaching car glared in her eyes, momentarily blinding her. She waved frantically, but it whizzed by.

Alicia was panting, her breath coming in shallow gasps. She ran on, driven only by fear, heading toward town.

Another car passed and Alicia waved again, but it didn't even slow down. We probably look insane, she thought, imagining the spectacle of her and Marta racing down the side of the highway.

No more cars passed. Soon Alicia reached the town and ran through the darkened streets.

The shops were all closed. The only light visible came from the streetlights. Even the carnival at the center of town was dark. It looked abandoned. Alicia ran toward it. She hoped that among the clutter of rides and booths, she would find a place to hide.

Alicia struggled to keep up the pace. As she ran she sometimes thought she actually felt Marta's breath on her neck.

Finally, she reached the carnival grounds. By now, her legs were nearly collapsing under her. She managed to get behind a ticket booth and leaned against it, gasping for air.

Where is Marta, she wondered warily. She knew she was there somewhere, lurking in the shadows, waiting to pounce. She strained her ears, listening for the sound of her footsteps. All she heard was the harsh rasping sound of her ragged breathing.

Then she felt someone grab her roughly by the collar, yanking her away from the booth, pulling her along.

Alicia lashed out blindly, but her hands only connected with air. She fought to keep from losing her balance as she stumbled along.

Then suddenly, the carousel lights went on, and the music began to play.

Chapter 24

The carousel was turning. The horses were going up and down, up and down, and the music was playing.

"Come on, Alicia, let's go, let's ride the horses!" It was Marta calling to her. She was about eight years old. Her dark brown hair hung in curls to her shoulders. She wore a maroon dress with white dots and a white collar. She was laughing.

"Just a minute! Wait! Let's wait for Cindy! I want her to come!" Alicia saw herself at age five, running away from the carousel. Her hair was cut very short, and she wore jeans and a T-shirt. I look like a little boy, she thought. I'm so small!

She looked back toward the carousel where Marta was standing and saw the little girl's smile disappear. A shadow seemed to fall across her face, darkening it from within. She looked older than her years, and positively menacing.

"No, Alicia! Come here! Why do you want Cindy to come? I want it to be just us!"

But the child Alicia wasn't paying any attention. She kept on running, calling, "Cindy! Cindy! Ride the carousel with us!"

Another child emerged from the crowd. She was about the same age as Alicia, with hair that was a mass of short, stiff, black curls. Alicia and the black-haired girl grabbed each other's hands and ran back toward the carousel. "C'mon, Cindy, it's going to start soon," Alicia said.

The two of them were near the carousel now, giggling as they ran. The man running the ride had his hand on the switch, shaking his head as he waited. They were almost there. . . .

"No! Don't go any farther!" Alicia shouted in her mind to the children. But they kept on running . . . and Marta had picked up a rock.

Alicia could see the whole scene as if it were happening before her eyes, even though it had been over ten years ago. "I don't want her to come with us!" Marta shouted as Cindy climbed onto the carousel.

Then everything happened in slow motion. Marta drew back her arm, and the rock struck Cindy on the shoulder, and she fell down, howling in pain.

Marta ran over and started pushing Alicia, all the time crying out, "See what you made me do! See what you made me do!"

Alicia had started to run away from her. Marta had chased after her yelling, "Stop it! I'm sorry! Come back, Alicia, and let's play sisters!"

The scene flashed into Alicia's mind with a white-hot burst of clarity and was gone. The lights from the carousel went out, the horses stopped moving, and the music died. The sunshine was gone and the darkness ruled once more. The full moon bathed the deserted carnival grounds in an eerie light.

Alicia's foot hit a rock as Marta pulled her along, sending sharp pain streaking through her foot and up along her leg. She lost her balance and her knee slammed hard into the ground.

Marta lost her grip on Alicia's collar. In an

instant, she turned around and was standing over her, reaching down toward her throat. From the look in her eyes, Alicia had no doubt that her childhood playmate had turned into someone who wanted to kill her.

Chapter 25

Alicia tried to twist away, but Marta got both hands around her neck. Marta jerked her head up and banged it back on to the ground.

"I'm sick of your being such an ungrateful sister." Marta hissed her words through her teeth, sounding like an angry snake. "If you want to get away from me so badly, I'll fix it so you'll get away for *good*."

Marta began squeezing Alicia's throat, her strong fingers digging into the flesh of her neck. Fighting for air, Alicia twisted her head to one side. It relieved some of the pressure on her neck for an instant. At the same time, she bent her knees and then kicked out with both feet, catching Marta squarely in the mid-section.

"*Gawww!*" Marta croaked as the air was knocked out of her. When she fell backward, a look of shocked surprise on her face, Alicia scrambled to her feet and began to run.

She didn't get very far before Marta was upon her again. Alicia felt the hands around her neck again, tightening. "I'm going to kill you." She growled the words into Alicia's ear.

Alicia struggled to pull away, but she was choking. Blackness was closing in from the edges of her vision. She felt as if she were falling, falling, into a deep, dark hole.

Behind Alicia, Marta's eyes bulged with effort as she squeezed tighter and tighter. She began shaking Alicia like a rag doll.

In a desperate attempt, Alicia stopped struggling and let herself go limp. Her knees buckled and she fell forward, bracing herself as she hit the ground with outstretched hands.

Caught off guard, Marta lost her balance and collapsed on the ground beside Alicia with a cry of surprise. Before Alicia could get to her feet, Marta reached and grabbed her left ankle in a viselike grip.

Putting all her strength behind it, Alicia drew back her right foot and kicked out as hard as she could. There was a sharp *thwack!* followed by a shriek of rage and pain as she struck Marta in the knee.

While Marta lay on the ground with her

hands clutching her knee, Alicia managed to scramble to her feet. She propelled herself over the ground in short, choppy strides. Marta yelled after her, and Alicia knew that Marta would quickly be up and in pursuit once more, driven by the maniacal desire to kill.

The carousel loomed before her. Afraid that if she tried to run around it, Marta would catch her, Alicia kept running straight on through the open gate and onto the carousel.

As soon as she had taken a few steps on the wooden boards, her heart sank. Her footsteps sounded so much louder than when she ran in the dirt and grass. It would be easy for Marta to know exactly where she was.

Her throat was hot and dry. She ducked behind one of the carousel animals and took several long gulps of air. She knew she had to keep moving, but she also knew she was exhausted and couldn't go on much longer.

Alicia's eyes darted this way and that in the darkness. Where was Marta? she asked herself.

In the split-second that she asked the question, Alicia felt a hand on her arm. She heard the hiss of angry breathing, and pulled away as if a hot iron had burned her.

Alicia ran, again dodging the shapes of the

carousel animals in the darkness. She ran with her hands groping in front of her, trying to keep from running into what she could not see. Behind her came the sound of Marta's footsteps and her labored breathing.

Then there was an explosion of light and sound. Suddenly the carousel was ablaze with light, and it moved to the eerie sound of a pump-organ melody.

For an instant Alicia's eyes were blinded by the lights. When she could make out the forms around her, she gasped at what she saw.

The carousel horses of her childhood were gone. They had been replaced by strange, grotesque animals painted in weird colors. *Gargoyles.*

The gargoyles danced to the music, up and down, up and down, their bulging eyes staring sightlessly into the night. But the most frightening expression didn't belong to one of the gargoyles. It was on Marta's face.

For an instant the two girls looked at each other. Then Marta lunged at Alicia, her features twisted into a grimace, her hands reaching out like claws.

Just as Marta was about to catch her, Alicia twisted to one side. Marta struck her hip on one of the gargoyles, and she shrieked in pain.

At the sound of Marta's scream, Alicia stiffened. Acting blindly, she turned and lashed out at Marta and hit her hard across the shoulders.

Still reeling from the shock of hitting her hip, Marta went down. Alicia heard a dull thud as Marta's head hit the boards of the carousel. Blinded by rage, Alicia prepared to hit her again. She knelt over Marta, her right hand curled in a fist, her teeth clenched together. She pulled back her arm, ready to strike. Then she realized that Marta wasn't moving.

Through the sound of the blood rushing through her head, Alicia heard people running toward the carousel. The lights on the Ferris wheel and several other rides blazed on one after the other. The entire carnival grounds were flooded with light in the middle of the darkened town. The effect was frightening and weirdly festive.

Alicia stood still, stunned by what was happening. Then she heard a voice that she knew was Mark's.

"Alicia, are you all right?"

The voice came from the direction of the Ferris wheel. Alicia ran toward it. Mark walked toward her. He was surrounded by police. "Where's Marta Taylor?" one of them asked, urgently.

"She's over there," Alicia said breathlessly, indicating the carousel. "Be careful. She's crazy."

"You're shivering," Mark said, embracing Alicia in his strong arms.

"She's crazy," Alicia repeated, leaning against him. "She's crazy."

"Don't worry," Mark said, holding her close. "The police will make sure she can't get at you."

Chapter 26

"When it comes to you, it seems my timing has always been off." Mark was sitting next to Alicia in the waiting room of the Grady County Hospital. She had spent the night there and been treated for her injuries. Now she awaited the arrival of her father.

"It's not *your* timing, Mark. It's just the way things are. . . ." Alicia's voice trailed off. She glanced at Jake Coyle, who sat across from them. He cleared his throat.

"Uh — I'm going to go get some coffee. I'll be back in about ten minutes. Your dad should be here by then." He hauled his large frame out of the chair and lumbered away.

Now only Alicia and Mark were left in the waiting room. Alicia spread out the newspaper clipping Jake had given her on the table.

Daughter of Famed Photojournalist Lyle

Fisher Missing, screamed the headlines. Following was a story about how Lyle Fisher had been away photographing wildlife in the Amazon jungle when he received word from his daughter's school that she had failed to attend for several days after the spring vacation. The spring vacation had lasted a week, and it had taken a few days to find Lyle Fisher in the jungle. It was unknown exactly how long his daughter had been missing. There was a photograph of Lyle Fisher and his daughter, Alicia.

"My mother died when I was ten. But Dad and I have always been close. He's probably been frantic."

Mark nodded. "I'll bet you can't wait to see him. You know, I was talking to the librarian this morning. It seems that Marta's parents died in a car accident a few months ago. The librarian said she noticed that Marta began acting stranger and stranger after that."

Alicia twisted her hands in her lap. "I guess that's what made her obsessed with the idea of having a sister. She wanted to have a family of some kind again. She was lonely. Even after everything that happened, I feel sorry for her."

Mark was silent for a moment. Then he

asked, "Will your father be bringing Lou with him?"

"He said he would."

"Are you sure everything's good between you and this Lou guy?" Mark asked, looking into her eyes. "Because if it isn't . . ."

"It *is*. We've been going together for two years. He goes to the same high school I do, we have the same interests, the same sense of humor, and . . ."

"Enough!" Mark said, faking a yawn. "I'm glad you're happy. I just don't want to hear about how great the guy is."

Alicia folded the clipping and put it in her pocket. "You've been a great friend, Mark. If it weren't for you, I might not even be here."

Mark shook his head. "I don't think so. I'm glad that I helped Jake Coyle find you, but I think you would have found a way out no matter what."

"I wonder . . . You know, I remember exactly how it all started. It was the last day of school before spring vacation. I stayed late in the art studio, working on a painting. It wasn't coming out the way I wanted, so I decided to leave it there over the break, and just work on some sketches at home."

Alicia felt a chill as she relived the scene in her mind. "That week, I thought I'd seen glimpses of Marta around school. Each time, though, she was gone before I could really get a look at her, so I thought I was mistaken. That night, when I went out to my car, I never suspected a thing.

"It was in the underpass that it happened. In my dreams I saw it as a tunnel. Suddenly, I saw a face in the rearview mirror. The eyes were blazing, and the face was wrapped in a black scarf. It looked like a vision from a nightmare."

"Alicia, you're shaking! Maybe you shouldn't talk about this now."

Alicia shook her head. "No, it's better that I talk about it. The more I talk about it, the more the fear will go away." She took a deep breath before continuing. "By the time I'd driven through the underpass, Marta had identified herself. She'd been hiding in the backseat, waiting for me. It didn't take long for me to realize that she was out of her mind, and I was really in trouble."

Mark stretched his long legs out in front of him, clasped his hands behind his head, and stared up at the ceiling. "I knew she was crazy.

I even thought she was capable of violence. But I never imagined her stalking someone and holding them prisoner. It's really incredible."

Alicia nodded. "I was so scared that I drove my car right into the woods. Somehow, I got away from Marta. Someone saw me wandering by the side of the road and called an ambulance." She looked into Mark's eyes. "Do you know they never even found my car? Marta must have . . . disposed of it somehow. Isn't that creepy?"

"Creepy," Mark said quietly. After a moment he looked at his watch. "I don't want to be around for the reunion with the boyfriend," he said, getting to his feet. "Listen, take care of yourself," he said. "And keep in touch."

"I will," Alicia said, softly. She watched as Mark walked away. He looks so lonely, Alicia thought, with a pang of sadness. She hoped he wouldn't feel too bad about her. He was such a nice guy.

A moment after Mark left, a young blond girl came in. She wore a name tag that read *Jana — Volunteer.* "Are you Ms. Fisher?"

Alicia nodded.

"Your father called. He had a flat tire — but he'll be here in about ten minutes." She turned to leave, hesitated, and turned back. "Do you know Mark Phillips, the guy that just left?"

"Yes. Do you know him, too?"

"Oh, sure." Jana's blond head nodded enthusiastically. She lowered herself into a chair beside Alicia and smiled as if they shared a secret. "He's a nice guy — but such an incredible flirt! Always after every girl, laying on the charm. Do you know what he told me? He said he had a crush on me since we were kids!"

"Really!" Alicia exclaimed, feeling indignant. Then, after a moment, she laughed. So, Mark was a regular Romeo, was he? And to think she'd been feeling sorry for him!

She and Jana chatted for a few minutes, then Jana left her alone to wait for her father and Lou. She kept looking at the clock as the minutes dragged by, each one seeming like an hour.

She heard a deep voice. "Thank goodness, you're all right."

"Dad! You're finally here!" Alicia jumped up and hugged the tall man with the wild, shaggy head of brown and silver hair. As she hugged him, she saw Lou over her father's shoulder.

In another moment, she was in Lou's arms.

They embraced without a word and held each other in silence for several moments. Alicia could feel his heart beating in his chest. Being in his arms felt like a dream come true.

Finally, the three of them sat down. "The administration of this hospital is going to find itself in deep trouble when I get started with them," Alicia's father said gruffly. "The idea that they accepted Marta's word that she was your sister without checking any identification whatsoever is outrageous! Your doctor had the nerve to whine to me that they're *busy* here!"

"I know, Dad, I know," Alicia agreed. "But let's not talk about it now, okay?"

Lou gave Alicia's hand a squeeze. "You'll never know how worried I was." He looked into her eyes. "I've been taking care of your canaries for you. They miss you. So do all of your friends."

"I miss them, too," Alicia said, leaning close to Lou. "But not as much as I missed you. You know, I never could believe Marta's description of me as a quiet girl who liked to stay home and do jigsaw puzzles."

Alicia's father and Lou looked at each other with startled expressions, and burst out laughing. "I should say not," Lou said, shaking his head.

After a moment, Alicia's father turned serious. "What happened to Marta?" he asked.

Alicia bit her lip. She had been trying not to think too much about it. But it haunted her. "They haven't found Marta," she whispered.

Chapter 27

Alicia looked out the window of the art studio at the Shelbyville High School of Art and Design. A month had passed since what she had come to refer to as *the incident*. Spring was in full bloom. Outside, she could see the pink and purple blossoms of the magnolia tree.

Alicia wiped her brush on a cloth. She had so much work to catch up on! Several days each week she stayed late, working in the studio alone on piece after piece.

Wiping her brush on a rag, Alicia stared at the canvas. The painting she was working on she called *Amnesia*. It was the *fifth* painting she had done called *Amnesia*.

"You'll work it out, and then you'll feel all right again. You've been through a lot, but you'll put it behind you," Lou said. Alicia hoped he was right. She just couldn't imagine a time when she'd feel as she did before it all happened.

It's so quiet here, she thought. Maybe I shouldn't have stayed so late. She listened for the sound of activity. There wasn't any.

It was nearly five o'clock, when they'd be locking the school doors. The maintenance man usually came at four-thirty to remind her they'd be closing. But this evening . . . he didn't.

Alicia felt a chill in the room. She raised her eyes, and shrieked.

Marta's eyes were blazing at her from the other side of the canvas.

"Look at this place! It's a mess!" she hissed. "Is this the way your sister taught you to keep your room?" Then she lunged at Alicia, knocking the painting to the floor.

"Oopsie daisy!"

Alicia shrieked again. Marta was holding the carving knife in her right hand.

"Don't be scared, Alicia," she said mockingly. "I was just going to fix you a sandwich."

Marta slashed the painting and the canvas tore with a sick, ripping sound. Then she charged at Alicia.

Too late, Alicia tried to run. Marta swung

her left hand in a wide arc and landed a blow on the side of Alicia's face. Pain exploded in Alicia's head as Marta struck her on the cheekbone. She saw an explosion of lights in front of her eyes as she fell to the ground.

She saw Marta's thick ankles as Marta stood over her body. Looking down at her, Marta's face twisted in a menacing grimace. Alicia saw the thin sheen of her teeth as Marta pulled her lips into a frightening grin.

Then, wordlessly, she drew the knife down Alicia's arm, slashing through the fabric of her flannel shirt. Horrified, Alicia saw Marta prepare to slash again. Then she passed out.

"Alicia, wake up! Alicia!" It was Lou's voice, she realized through a haze.

"Alicia!" Lou said again. Alicia blinked and stared up at his face. She was lying on the floor of the studio, and Lou was cradling her head in his arms. Fred, the maintenance man, was with him.

Alicia jerked into a sitting position. "Where has Marta gone? She was here! She slashed the painting! Look — she cut my shirt with a knife!"

Lou and Fred didn't move. They just looked at each other.

"Well, do something!" Alicia urged. "She'll come after me again!"

Lou and Fred didn't move. Then Alicia saw her painting. It was sitting on the easel, unharmed.

"When I came in, you were unconscious, and your painting was on the floor. I picked it up. It doesn't look like it's damaged."

Then Alicia looked at her arm. The sleeve of her shirt wasn't ripped. She hadn't been cut at all.

Lou pulled her close for a moment. Then he looked at her solemnly. "Marta couldn't have been here, Alicia. They found her a few days after your father and I picked you up, remember? She's in a mental hospital miles and miles from here."

It was true.

"I think I'm going crazy myself," Alicia murmured. "I keep thinking I see her, and it's so real!"

"I think I spooked you," said Fred. "I was so busy I forgot to remind you we were closing, and then when I came in I kept talking to you — but you acted like you didn't hear me. Then I came around behind the canvas and looked at you — and you started screaming."

"I thought I saw Marta," Alicia said. "I imagined the whole thing! Oh, Lou, I'm losing my mind!"

"Shh! Shhh! That's not true," Lou said, gently. "You went through a terrifying experience. You're still scared, that's all. You'll get through this thing, I know you will. I believe in you."

"I'm sorry I scared you," said Fred, sounding embarrassed. "Uh — your painting's okay, though, so you can finish it."

Alicia got to her feet and looked at the murky swirls of color. "No, I don't think I will," she said after a moment. "I think I'll start something new — and different. Maybe that's a good way to start putting the whole experience behind me."

"I'm glad to hear you say that," Lou said, his black eyes shining as he smiled at her. "In fact, I think we should go somewhere and celebrate."

"Great idea." Alicia smiled back at him. Holding hands, they left the studio and walked down the empty corridor toward the door.

Alone in the studio, Fred stared at Alicia's painting for a moment. "Abstract art," he mumbled, shaking his head. "Weird." Then he shrugged, and turned off the light.

THRILLERS

D.E. Athkins
- ☐ MC45246-0 Mirror, Mirror $3.25
- ☐ MC45349-1 The Ripper $3.25

A. Bates
- ☐ MC45829-9 The Dead Game $3.25
- ☐ MC43291-5 Final Exam $3.25
- ☐ MC44582-0 Mother's Helper $3.25
- ☐ MC44238-4 Party Line $3.25

Caroline B. Cooney
- ☐ MC44316-X The Cheerleader $3.25
- ☐ MC41641-3 The Fire $3.25
- ☐ MC43806-9 The Fog $3.25
- ☐ MC45681-4 Freeze Tag $3.25
- ☐ MC45402-1 The Perfume $3.25
- ☐ MC44884-6 The Return of the Vampire $2.95
- ☐ MC41640-5 The Snow $3.99
- ☐ MC45680-6 The Stranger $3.50
- ☐ MC45682-2 The Vampire's Promise $3.50

Richie Tankersley Cusick
- ☐ MC43115-3 April Fools $3.25
- ☐ MC43203-6 The Lifeguard $3.25
- ☐ MC43114-5 Teacher's Pet $3.25
- ☐ MC44235-X Trick or Treat $3.50

Carol Ellis
- ☐ MC46411-6 Camp Fear $3.25
- ☐ MC44768-8 My Secret Admirer $3.25
- ☐ MC47101-5 Silent Witness $3.25
- ☐ MC46044-7 The Stepdaughter $3.25
- ☐ MC44916-8 The Window $3.25

Lael Littke
- ☐ MC44237-6 Prom Dress $3.50

Jane McFann
- ☐ MC46690-9 Be Mine $3.25

Christopher Pike
- ☐ MC43014-9 Slumber Party $3.50
- ☐ MC44256-2 Weekend $3.50

Edited by T. Pines
- ☐ MC45256-8 Thirteen $3.99

Sinclair Smith
- ☐ MC45063-8 The Waitress $3.50

Barbara Steiner
- ☐ MC46425-6 The Phantom $3.50

Robert Westall
- ☐ MC41693-6 Ghost Abbey $3.25
- ☐ MC43761-5 The Promise $3.25
- ☐ MC45176-6 Yaxley's Cat $3.25

Available wherever you buy books, or use this order form.